ESSENCE OF THE WITCH

WITCHES OF KEATING HOLLOW, BOOK 8

DEANNA CHASE

Copyright © 2019 by Deanna Chase

Editing: Angie Ramey

Cover image: © Ravven

ISBN Print 978-1-940299-97-6

ISBN Ebook 978-1-940299-96-9

Bayou Moon Press, LLC

www.deannachase.com

Printed in the United States of America

ABOUT THIS BOOK

Miranda Moon has been cursed. Ever since she had the misfortune to come in contact with a crude love spell, she's had one bad date after another. After lighting a man's hair on fire and ending up on a blind date with her cousin, she's ready to lose herself in the books she writes and live her life as a spinster… until Gideon Alexander, the one man she's always wanted, walks back into her life.

Gideon Alexander doesn't date. He's already found the one and lost her. But when he's asked to plan the Keating Hollow Christmas ball with his old flame Miranda Moon, suddenly he finds himself breaking his own rules. Maybe dating the sexy author is just what his scarred heart needs. The only problem? Miranda's curse has the potential to destroy their relationship before it ever begins.

CHAPTER 1

*B*utterflies fluttered in Miranda Moon's stomach as she stood in front of the Cozy Cave restaurant and steeled herself for the blind date Jacob Burton had sprung on her two hours ago. If Jacob hadn't been one of her oldest friends, there was no way she would've caved and agreed to this date. She wasn't so desperate that she needed to drop everything just to get dinner with a man. Even if that man was a respected screenwriter who happened to have written her favorite movie of all time.

Okay, she would've definitely caved. Who passed up a date with Cameron Copeland, the creator of *Endless Shades of Midnight*, the most romantic movie ever filmed? But she would've insisted on more than two hours' notice. It usually took her that long just to settle on an outfit.

Miranda glanced down at her black-lace corset dress and second-guessed her choice. Maybe she should've worn the cream version with violet ribbons. It was decidedly more romantic and probably more appropriate for a date.

She let out a groan. If Cameron Copeland didn't like her

because she wore all black, a relationship would never work anyway. More than half her wardrobe was black.

"Miranda?" a woman called from behind her.

She turned and spotted Shannon Ansell, a tall redhead wearing a green wool dress and gorgeous black boots. It was a far cry from the jeans, T-shirt, and apron she wore every day at A Spoonful of Magic, the shop Miranda often frequented while getting in her daily word count for whatever book she was working on at the moment. "Shannon. Hey. Are you meeting Brian for dinner?"

Shannon shook her head and smiled wide. "Nope. Hope, Yvette, Faith, and I are having girls' night out while Brian and Jacob entertain Skye."

Skye was Jacob's little girl he was raising with Yvette. And Brian, Shannon's fiancé, was the toddler's godfather. "I'm sure they'll have a good time." The two men were best friends, and both of them loved that little girl with a fierceness Miranda envied. Her own father had never had much interest in her when she was a child.

"Not as good a time as we're going to have. We have big plans for margaritas," Shannon said with a wry grin. "Everything is more fun with tequila."

"I can't argue with that, I guess." Miranda laughed but had trouble picturing them downing margaritas on the chilly December night. If it were her, she'd be ordering Irish coffees instead of icy cocktails.

"Congratulations by the way! You must be so excited." Shannon beamed at her.

"Um, sure?" Did Shannon just congratulate her on landing a date with Cameron Copeland? That seemed... odd. Shannon wasn't usually the excitable type, and she sure didn't swoon over the opposite sex or celebrities. She was

ESSENCE OF THE WITCH

more of a roll-her-eyes kind of girl until a guy proved he wasn't going to be a complete douchebucket.

Shannon's eyebrows shot up. "Sure? That's a little subdued even for you, don't you think? It's not every day someone's book gets made into a movie."

"Oh, that." Miranda shrugged, wondering if Yvette had said something about the deal she'd made with Witching Hour Productions. But that had been months ago, and Miranda hadn't really talked about it since her last book signing at Hollow Books, the local bookstore that Jacob and Yvette owned. "Don't get too excited. Movie options on books very rarely go anywhere."

Shannon jerked back as surprise filtered through her green gaze. "You haven't heard yet, have you?"

"Heard what?" Miranda's skin started to tingle with a hint of excitement. Shannon's brother was a young Hollywood star, and she'd recently started to manage his career. She had connections that could put her in the position to know if a project was getting off the ground. "What do you know?"

A huge grin claimed Shannon's lips as her eyes sparkled with excitement. "Witching Hour wants Silas to play Mandy's best friend. They're talking about starting production this summer."

Miranda's breath left her as shock rooted her to the spot on the brick sidewalk. She forced air into her lungs and then whispered, "You can't be serious. You are. Aren't you? They really are moving forward with *Witching for You?*"

"Yes. They really are."

"Oh my goddess. That's... crazy." Excitement mixed with pure panic rushed through Miranda. *Witching for You* was the first book she ever wrote and was based on her first love. She'd changed a lot of the details, but the heart of the story was all about her relationship with her college boyfriend. When she sold the rights, she hadn't ever really thought a movie would be made, so she hadn't considered what it might feel like to have her story up on the silver screen. It was both exhilarating and terrifying.

"I can't believe you didn't know this. Isn't that information that your agent should've passed on to you?" Shannon asked.

Miranda snapped out of her daze and let out a humorless chuckle. "She might have if we hadn't broken up earlier this year. She was upset that I didn't take the last deal we were offered. The publisher lowballed me, so I just published it myself. She wasn't thrilled and told me I should find someone new."

"Whoa." Shannon frowned. "I'm sorry. That must've been hard."

Miranda waved an unconcerned hand. "It doesn't matter. She was pushing me to do something that wasn't in my best interest, and that's not someone I want working for me. It's fine. Except now I'm going to need to contact her about the movie. If they are moving into production, that means I'll be due some extra funds." Miranda stepped closer to Shannon and wrapped her in a hug. "Thank you. This is fantastic news."

Shannon squeezed her tightly. "You deserve this. *Witching for You* is a wonderful book."

"Thanks." Tears stung Miranda's eyes, but she let out a laugh, and as she pulled away, she wiped at her eyes. "I can't believe I'm so emotional about this."

"It's a big deal. This time next year you could be famous." Shannon winked.

Miranda grimaced. "Oh, no. Don't wish that on me. I just want to hide out here in Keating Hollow and write."

Shannon smirked. "You're not the only one."

Miranda was about to ask what she meant by that, but then Shannon swept her gaze over Miranda and said, "You look really good in that dress. Who are *you* meeting for dinner?"

"Jacob didn't tell you?" Miranda asked, surprised that half the town didn't already know that Cameron Copeland had landed in Keating Hollow.

Shannon shook her head. "Nope." She leaned in closer and whispered, "Now spill."

The wind picked up, chilling Miranda to the bone, and she clutched her wrap around her, trying to stave off the cold. "Blind date with a screenwriter. Cameron Copeland."

Shannon's eyes went wide again. "You're having dinner with Cameron?"

Miranda tilted her head to the side. "Do you know him?"

"Yeah. We've met. Brian and I had dinner with him a few weeks ago when we were down in Los Angeles to visit Brian's parents. Since then, Cameron has been talking about writing something for Silas as the lead, so we've been in contact." She pursed her lips. "Hmm. In fact, Silas was supposed to hear from him sometime today. I wonder if they ever connected." She pulled out her phone and sent a text. She got a response almost instantly, causing her to roll her eyes. When she glanced up, she said, "I think your date is going to be late."

Miranda let out a sigh. Of course he was. All of her dates lately had been a complete disaster. The last one had ended up being a blind date with her cousin. Her stomach rolled just thinking about it. An author friend had set her up with her husband's college buddy who turned out to be Perry, her second cousin on her mother's side. Even if they hadn't been related, the date would've been a total loss. Perry was an uptight businessman who thought Miranda was a flighty, free spirit who needed to grow up and get a real job. As if writing wasn't a real job. She was still steamed every time she thought of his condescending tone.

"Is Cameron meeting with Silas right now?" Miranda asked her friend.

"It looks like it. Do you want to join me and the girls for dinner instead?" Shannon asked.

"Miranda?" A tall man with dark curly hair called out as he strode toward them. "Miranda Moon?"

"Yes?" she said as she turned and stared at the gorgeous specimen. He had brilliant aqua eyes, a lean but muscular frame, and an angular jaw that was to die for. With his sexy five o'clock shadow, he looked like he belonged on the cover of *GQ*.

"Hi." He gave her a shy but oh-so-sexy half smile and held out his hand. "I'm Jax, Cameron's assistant. He was unavoidably detained and asked me to step in for him and take you to dinner. I know I'm not who you were expecting, but if you're game I'd love to share a meal with a gorgeous and talented writer."

"Um…" Miranda started.

"She'd love to," Shannon blurted and then nudged Miranda toward the beautiful man. "I recommend the seafood risotto."

"Sounds fantastic." Jax held his arm out to Miranda. "What do you say, Miranda? Are you ready?"

Miranda was speechless as she stared at him, her mouth dry. Had she ever seen a man so handsome before? With her

6

luck, he was probably married already and just doing his boss a favor. Still, she'd gotten dressed up and was starving. If this lovely creature wanted to buy her a meal, she wasn't going to say no. She flashed him a smile as she wrapped her arm around his. "Sure. Just as long as there's wine."

He laughed and started to lead her toward the restaurant's door. "I think we're going to get along just fine."

Miranda glanced back at Shannon. "Thanks for the information. See you tomorrow at the shop?"

Shannon nodded and gave her a big thumbs-up as she mouthed, *He's hot. Take that one home tonight.*

Miranda rolled her eyes but decided her friend had a point and silently prayed that her dating luck was about to change.

CHAPTER 2

*G*ideon Alexander sat at a table in the back of the restaurant and glanced down when his phone pinged with an incoming message. It was the fifth one in an hour from his father's assistant. Instead of answering, he gritted his teeth, forwarded the texts to his own assistant with a note reiterating that he'd be unavailable for the next week, and then turned the thing off.

When was the last time he'd taken a real vacation? One that didn't involve multiple conference calls and a dozen urgent emails a day? Never. But this time was going to be different. If he didn't slow down and enjoy life a little, then what exactly had he been working toward the last fifteen years?

Sitting back in his chair, Gideon took a sip of his wine as his gaze swept over the quaint restaurant. The Cozy Cave was his favorite kind of eatery. The farm-to-table establishment had new daily offerings but was unpretentious with its mix-n-match place settings and casual atmosphere. It was a refreshing change from the fancy, high-end dining he was always roped into down in Los Angeles. The waiter arrived and took his order for ricotta cheese- and pesto-stuffed trout and a cranberry and walnut salad. His stomach rumbled with anticipation, and just as he reached for the fresh sourdough bread, his gaze landed on the most beautiful woman he'd ever seen.

The one he'd been dreaming about on and off for the last fifteen years.

He dropped the bread and leaned in, eyeing her. She had long, dark, shiny curls that framed a gorgeous heart-shaped face. And dammit if she wasn't wearing a form-fitting dress that showed off all of her luscious curves. His mouth went dry and he blinked, wondering if he was seeing things.

Nope. She wasn't an illusion. Miranda Moon, the woman he'd fallen in love with back in college, was right there only ten feet away on the arm of a younger man who looked all too familiar. Gideon was certain he knew him from somewhere; he just couldn't place him. An actor maybe? He certainly was good looking enough.

His stomach clenched with the unmistakable signs of jealousy.

Son of a... Gideon had zero claim on Miranda. He'd been the one who'd walked away from her years ago. She'd been heartbroken, but what she'd never known was just how much he'd regretted it. At the time, he'd thought he had no choice. Now? What had he left her for? To make his father happy? To build a high-powered career in the film industry that was mostly about writing checks and had little to do with his artistic vision?

Gideon sighed and imagined what his life might be like if he'd defied his father and followed his heart. The vision was filled with Miranda, barefoot in a tiny sun-filled apartment, and a lot of laughter. What it didn't have was a fancy house in Malibu or a shiny black sports car that never left his garage. He let out a humorless chuckle. There was no doubt he'd give up both in a hot second if he could go back and change things. But he couldn't rewrite history. He knew that better than anyone.

A waiter appeared, cutting off his view of Miranda as he placed Gideon's salad in front of him. "Can I get you anything else, Mr. Alexander? Another glass of wine?"

Gideon eyed his empty glass, surprise filtering through him. He didn't remember draining the glass. "Yes, please."

The waiter nodded and took off back to the bar while Gideon let his gaze fixate on Miranda again. Her face lit up with a smile at something the man said, making his gut twist. He wanted to be sitting at that table with her. What would happen if he got up and went over and said hello? Would she be happy to see him, or would she be angry?

Gideon shook his head. How silly it was to think she would be angry. They'd broken up years ago. There was no doubt she'd gotten over him. Was he so egotistical that he thought she might've been pining for him all these years? Hell, he hadn't been pining for her. Not really. He'd always thought of her as the one who got away, but it wasn't as if he'd devoted any time to trying to find her. And yet there he was, unable to keep is eyes off her, his undeniable desire for her just as strong as it had been fifteen years ago.

He couldn't let this moment pass him by without at least saying hello. Or getting her number. They'd been close once. They could catch up on each other's lives, right? Gideon's gaze locked on Miranda's hands as he searched for a wedding ring. He frowned when he realized there was no way to easily tell if she was married. Almost every finger bore some sort of ring, just as they always had.

Screw it, he thought as he pushed his chair back and rose to his feet. There was no time like the present. If he let this moment go, he knew he'd regret it for the rest of his life. Straightening his shoulders, he adjusted the suit coat he'd worn to his meeting that morning before hopping the plane to Eureka, the nearest airport. He felt like a corporate drone, lightyears away from the man she'd known way back then. Gideon imagined that after they parted ways again she'd have a good laugh at what he'd become. The idealist artist who'd wanted nothing more than to open his own gallery in a beachside tourist town had long been buried by the bean counter who held the purse strings for a major media company.

Miranda's eyes danced as she said something to her dinner companion. He was clearly delighted with her as he threw his head back and laughed. It was then he noticed the other man had his hand covering hers. Gideon's gaze fixated on the connection, and he gritted his teeth but then forced himself to unclench his jaw as he neared the table and turned his attention back to her. She hadn't yet noticed him, which was a good thing since he was certain his emotions had been lining his face. *Get it together, man,* he ordered himself and pasted on a smile he'd perfected over his years of business meetings.

"Miranda?" He gripped the back of an empty chair and smiled down at her.

She froze for just a moment before jerking her head to stare up at him, shock clouding her lovely dark chocolate-colored eyes. Her voice was barely a whisper as she said, "Gideon?"

A smile tugged at his lips. "Surprise."

She jumped and yanked her hand from the man's as if she'd been caught by a lover on an illicit date. In her haste, her hand collided with a pillar candle in the middle of the table, and as she reached to steady it, she missed, sending the thing straight at her date. He'd been reaching forward to help her with his head much too close to the flame, and as the candle flew past him, suddenly his hair went up in flames.

"Oh no!" Miranda reached for her water glass and threw it at him, drenching his face but missing his hair.

The man let out a shout and patted his head as he jumped up and turned toward the restrooms.

"Stop!" Gideon demanded, already reaching for the magic tingling in his veins.

Her date froze as if Gideon's command had magically compelled him in some way. Gideon knew that was impossible; he didn't have that type of power. But he could do something about the fire. With just one hand on the man's head and a snap of his fingers, the fire vanished, leaving the man with charred ends and the rancid scent of burnt hair filling Gideon's nose.

The other man sank into a chair, covering his head with both hands and breathing hard. "Holy hell," he muttered. "That was... crazy."

"Oh my goodness, sir. Are you all right?" the waiter asked, crouching down beside the man. "Do we need to call an ambulance?"

Gideon could've told the young waiter that was unnecessary. The fire had been clinging to whatever hair product the man had used, and Gideon had put it out before any real damage occurred.

"No. No," the man said, shaking his head. "I'm fine. I just... wow. That was crazy."

"Jax!" Miranda finally shook herself out of her shocked state. "I'm so sorry. I can't believe I did that." She took a good look at him and winced. "Your hair. Oh, man. I can't apologize enough."

Jax ran his hands over his hair again, his eyes going wide with a dawning realization. "I have to go." He stood quickly. "I can't believe this. I have a modeling shoot next week. I have to get this fixed." Jax took off for the door. After a few steps, he paused and glanced over his shoulder. "I'd say it was nice to meet you, Miranda, but this is just... Son of a... *dammit*. If I show up at my shoot like this, I'm going to be fired. Thanks for nothing."

Miranda apologized again, but Jax ran out of the restaurant, muttering to himself about needing a new job and how he was done schmoozing for his boss.

"That was exciting," Gideon said, taking Jax's abandoned seat.

Miranda blinked at him as if she were trying to decide if he was real or not.

He smiled at her. "It's good to see you again."

"Gideon," she finally breathed out. Then her expression turned hard and angry as she said, "What are you doing here?"

Jerking back, it was Gideon's turn to blink at her. Her anger left him momentarily speechless. She couldn't still be holding a grudge after all those years, could she? But judging by her narrowed eyes and the sneer claiming her lips, that was exactly what was happening here. "Here at the restaurant or here in Keating Hollow?" he asked just to bide time.

Her dark eyes turned almost black. "Both."

Someone who didn't know her well might be intimidated by the anger rolling off her, but the Miranda he'd known used anger to mask a whole host of emotions. If he had to guess, he'd say there was a lot of fear lurking under that expression. But fear of what? Him? He was the last person she needed to worry about.

"Well?" she pressed, leaning back and crossing her arms over her chest.

He cleared his throat. "I'm here in Keating Hollow on vacation, and this is the first restaurant I saw this afternoon when I rolled into town." Gideon eyed her thoughtfully. "What about you? What brings you to Keating Hollow?"

She gave him a flat stare. "I live here."

His lips curved into a grin. "Well, then. Looks like I might have to extend my trip a few weeks."

CHAPTER 3

*W*hat *in the fresh pumpkin spice was happening right now?* In addition to being mortified about setting Jax's hair on fire, Miranda was completely thrown by the sudden appearance of Gideon Alexander.

The moment she'd laid eyes on him her heart swelled, and pure joy filled all of her empty spaces. He was just as handsome as he'd been in college, with wavy brown hair, piercing blue eyes, and a body that looked like it belonged to an athlete. Only he'd gotten his muscles in his workshop instead of a gym. Did that mean he was still sculpting? She hoped so, but she also knew he'd left that part of him behind when he'd gone to work for his father's company.

How many times had she imagined running into him again? Hundreds at least. But never once had that vision included her fumbling a candle and nearly sending a guy up in flames. As the embarrassment kicked in, so did the suspicion. It couldn't be a coincidence that he'd shown up in Keating Hollow at the exact same time that her book was finally being made into a movie... the book that was written about their relationship. It was also the book that had almost never been published because the media company his father owned tried to bury it.

Was he in Keating Hollow to try to stop the movie? She wasn't sure how he could since she'd sold the rights to Witching Hour Productions, a rival media company, but there was a reason people always said that everyone and everything had a price.

Miranda hadn't actually thought he'd been involved in trying to bury her book. She'd always assumed that honor went to Gideon's father, whom she'd always known was no fan of hers. But considering there was talk of Witching Hour moving forward with her movie, why else would he suddenly show up after all these years? All of the joy she'd felt earlier vanished, and all she saw was red as she grilled him. "You just happened to choose Keating Hollow for a vacation? Really? The town is out-of-the-way and tiny. Don't you vacation in places like Hawaii or something?"

Gideon placed his elbows on the table and leaned in. "Miranda, I don't vacation."

She raised one eyebrow. He didn't know it, but he'd just given a piece of evidence to support her theory. If he didn't vacation, why else was he in her town? "You're here, aren't you?"

His lips twitched before he said, "It seems so."

Why was he so effing smug? Miranda wanted to wipe that tiny smile right off his face while also wanting to lean in and... what? Kiss him? That's what flashed through her mind, and she hated herself for it. He left her fifteen years ago. His company tried to stop the publication of her first book. He'd not only crushed her heart, but someone in his orbit had tried to crush her dreams, too. She stood. "I can't do this."

A flicker of something that looked an awful lot like alarm flashed through his eyes. He jumped up and reached out to place a hand on her arm. "Miranda, wait."

"For what? For you to rip my heart out again?" she spat out. Then she closed her eyes, hating how bitter and lovesick that sounded. It had been *years*. She was over him. She had to be. "You know what? Never mind." Embarrassed and completely mortified, Miranda grabbed her wrap and rushed to the hostess stand. "I need to pay the check for my table, please."

"I've got it." Gideon's voice sounded from right behind her.

Miranda whirled around. "I can't let you do that."

He handed the hostess his credit card. "Sure, you can. It's the least I can do after ruining your evening. I'm really sorry, Miranda. All I wanted to do was say hello. I can see that was a mistake. Don't worry. I'll stay out of your hair while I'm here in town."

"I bet," she muttered and stalked out of the restaurant. But as soon as she got outside, she started to feel like a complete jerk. She'd totally bitten his head off and hadn't even thanked him for paying for the meals neither she nor Jax had eaten.

A gust of wind blew, chilling her to the bone, and she took a minute to cloak herself in her wrap. She had to go back in there and apologize. She'd made a bunch of assumptions, but the man hadn't done anything but try to be friendly.

"Crap," she said under her breath and reached for the door. But before she could wrap her hand around the handle, the door swung open and Gideon stepped out onto the cobbled sidewalk.

"Miranda. You're still here," he said, sounding surprised.

"Um. Yeah." She wrapped her arms around herself, trying to keep warm in the early December evening. "I was headed back in to find you."

He frowned and actually took a step back.

She couldn't blame him. She'd likely do the same thing if he'd treated her the way she'd treated him. "I'm sorry," she said. "I shouldn't have barked at you, and you certainly didn't deserve to have your head bitten off. I didn't mean it. I think I was just taken by surprise and a little out of my mind after what happened to Jax."

Gideon didn't say anything for a few beats, but then he held out the plastic bag he was holding. "Here. This is the dinner you and Jax didn't get to eat."

She stared at the plastic bag and then shook her head. "Thanks, but you paid for it. You should take it with you for a late dinner or lunch tomorrow."

He chuckled and placed the bag in her hand. "I'm good, Miranda. Please take your dinner home. I've done enough to disrupt your evening." She opened her mouth to protest, but he held a hand up and said, "Why don't we just leave it here tonight. We've both apologized. No hard feelings, huh?"

Miranda just nodded because she didn't know what else to do. She still had her suspicions about why he might be in town, but that's all they were... suspicions. Maybe he had come to town for a short vacation. Keating Hollow had been put on the map a few months ago when the paparazzi had followed Silas Ansell back to his hometown. It wasn't exactly that far-fetched that a fire witch would seek some R & R in a magical village. It was time to shake off her paranoia.

"Thanks, Gideon. That was kind of you," she said, leaning in to kiss him on the cheek. But Gideon moved at the last second, and she ended up brushing a light kiss over his lips. A shiver ghosted over her skin as tiny bells went off in her head, proving once and for all that she hadn't gotten over him. It had been fifteen years, and he still had the same effect on her that he did in college.

"Goodnight, Miranda," he said softly. And then he turned and strode away.

Miranda watched him until he climbed into a black SUV and disappeared down Main Street.

"THE END!" Miranda called out and raised her arms over her head in a victory motion.

"The end?" Shannon asked, her voice skeptical. "What did you do? Cut off five thousand words from your wordcount goal?"

Miranda glanced over at her friend behind the counter at A Spoonful of Magic and flashed what she assumed was a manic smile. What else could it be? She'd just written over twelve thousand words in one day while she sat at a table inside the confectionary shop. "Nope. I even went over a couple thousand."

"Dang, girl. This calls for a celebration." Shannon strode out from behind the counter and held her hand out to Miranda. "Get out of that chair before you develop a blood clot and let's go to Incantation Café for some of Hanna's gingerbread cookies and Irish coffees."

"Wait. The Incantation Café has started serving alcohol?"

Miranda asked after the mention of Irish coffees perked her up.

"Nope." Shannon laughed. "But I happen to know Hanna keeps a bottle of Irish cream in the fridge."

"I knew I liked her." Miranda took Shannon's hand and let the other woman pull her out of the chair. Her back and legs were so stiff that she had trouble just standing up straight. "Hold on. I think I need a minute."

Shannon shook her head. "I told you your butt was gonna grow roots. I think you only got up once to go to the bathroom. Good thing you didn't have your regular six cups of coffee today, or your bladder would've given out on you."

Miranda laughed. "I was on a roll. You don't mess with that."

"I guess not."

After taking a moment to stretch her achy limbs, Miranda packed up her laptop and followed Shannon to the door. When she flicked the lights off and locked the door behind them, Miranda glanced at her phone. "It's closing time already?"

Shannon gave her a patient smile. "Closing time was an hour ago."

"What?" Miranda pulled her wool coat around her tighter and gaped at Shannon. "Why didn't you kick me out?"

"I tried, but you wouldn't budge." She winked at Miranda. "Just kidding. I did mention it was closing time. You were so engrossed in what you were writing that you didn't even look at me. I had some paperwork to do, so I just decided to leave you be while I finished up."

Miranda slipped her arm through Shannon's and leaned her head against the other woman's shoulder. "You're the best. You know that, right?"

"Yep." She brushed imaginary dust from her shoulders, and they both laughed as they made their way into Incantation Café.

When they were seated near the fireplace with their secret Irish coffee's, Shannon fixed her gaze on Miranda and said, "Okay, spill. And I want all the dirty details. How do you know Gideon Alexander, and what is he doing here in Keating Hollow?"

Miranda put her coffee mug down and tilted her head. "I, uh, was going to ask you the same thing. About what he's doing here, I mean."

"I have no idea," Shannon said, appearing sincere as she leaned back and pursed her lips. "Honestly, I've met with producers before, and even some from his media company, but not him."

Miranda let her gaze drop to her coffee mug as she said, "I kind of thought he might be here about *Witching for You.*"

"You did?"

When Miranda glanced back up at her, Shannon's expression was confused. "Well, yeah. Why else would he be here? He said he came for vacation, but why would he come here? His family has more money than the Queen of England. Gideon could literally go anywhere."

"Ace Media isn't involved with *Witching for You,*" Shannon said. "Witching Hour doesn't partner with them. Did you hear something?"

That sinking feeling Miranda had the night before when she'd jumped to conclusions about Gideon came rushing back. She'd had all night to think it through, and she'd still come to the tentative conclusion that he must've been in town to derail her movie. "No. Nothing like that. I just…"

She blew out a breath and met Shannon's eyes. "About those dirty details you wanted…"

"Yes?" Shannon said when Miranda didn't elaborate.

"*Witching for You* is about me and Gideon. He was my college boyfriend. I thought maybe… Well, I guess I thought he was trying to get the movie stopped or something in case anyone realizes the male lead is based on him."

"Whoa."

"Yeah. Whoa." Miranda took a big gulp of her Irish coffee, already contemplating a second cup.

"Do you really think he'd do that?" Shannon asked. "I haven't heard of any complications. In fact, Silas and I are anticipating a contract later this week. The initial negotiations are already hammered out."

"Really?" Miranda's stomach flipped with nerves and anticipation. "That sounds like things are really happening."

Shannon gave her a gentle smile. "It does. Anything could happen of course, even once they start filming, but if contracts are being handed out, that means the production company is serious. They'll have to pay either way once they're signed. They don't like to pay out on projects that go nowhere. Especially Witching Hour. They have a good track record of follow-through."

"That's good to hear." That ball of unease returned to Miranda's gut as she thought of the night before and how she'd behaved with Gideon. She'd been a complete idiot in more ways than one. "I should probably find him and apologize again. I was kind of rude."

"You, rude?" Shannon asked with a chuckle. "I find that hard to believe. A little forward or blunt maybe, but rude isn't how I would describe you."

Miranda winced. "You might've seen us there, but you

didn't hear what I said. There's a lot of unresolved history there."

"I bet." She shifted her gaze over Miranda's shoulder and then nodded toward the door. "Here's your chance. Looks like we're not the only ones who needed a late afternoon shot of caffeine."

Miranda quickly glanced over her shoulder and spotted Gideon making his way toward the front counter. Her body tensed, and those damned butterflies were back in her gut. Shannon was right. This was her chance to talk to him. The only problem was that she wasn't sure she could do it without being a bumbling idiot.

"I need to get going," Shannon said. "Brian and Silas will be waiting on me for dinner."

As the other woman stood, Miranda reached out and grabbed her hand, squeezing slightly. "Thanks, Shannon. You're a good friend."

Shannon grinned down at her. "I am, aren't I?"

Miranda laughed. "I see you aren't lacking ego either."

"Only when I'm having a bad hair day." She winked. "Listen. Hope, Hanna, and I are planning another girls' night tomorrow night. Are you interested? The three of us were thinking mani-pedis at Faith's spa and then dinner at the Townsend Brewery."

A night out with the girls? There was no way she was going to turn that down. She hadn't lived in Keating Hollow long, and while she was friendly with Yvette and her sisters as well as Shannon, she hadn't made much of an effort in the friend department. It was time to change that. "Sure. What time?"

Shannon gave her the details and glanced one last time at Gideon, who was now settled at a table near the front window. "Good luck with that one. If the apology doesn't work, try flashing him some leg. I never met a man who could resist a little bit of skin."

Miranda rolled her eyes, but she knew Shannon was only teasing. She showed appreciation for Miranda's fondness for wearing dresses all the time. Especially the ones that revealed a little skin.

"They're just so... you," Shannon said. "Sexy, romantic, alluring. Just like your books."

"Thank you," Miranda said, her cheeks heating with a flush. "That's kind."

"It's the truth," Shannon said. "See you tomorrow."

As Shannon made her way out of the café, Miranda took a deep breath and walked over to Gideon. When he glanced up at the sound of her footsteps, she asked, "Is this seat taken?"

CHAPTER 4

"$\mathcal{I}$ t is now," Gideon said, gazing up at the beauty he hadn't been able to get out of his mind since he'd seen her the night before. It had taken all of his willpower to not follow her home or try to get her number. After her reaction to him and her outburst about him leaving her, he'd thought it best to just leave things alone. He wasn't interested in upsetting her further just by being present. But now that she'd approached him, there was no way he was going to turn her away.

She gave him a sheepish smile. "I know I already apologized for my behavior last night, but I feel like a complete jerk. Will you let me take you out to dinner while you're in town to make it up to you? Assuming you have time, of course."

"You don't need to make anything up to me, Miranda. But I'd love to have dinner with you." His lips twitched, and he couldn't help the smile that claimed them. She'd just given him an opening he couldn't refuse. "I have nothing but time. How about tonight? Tomorrow? Both?"

"Both?" she asked, raising a skeptical eyebrow, making sure he knew she thought he was pushing his luck. He didn't care though. While he was in Keating Hollow, it would be impossible to stay away from her. "Maybe just tonight," she finally said. "Tomorrow I have plans."

He raised his coffee cup in a one-sided toast. "It's a date then."

Miranda glanced down at herself, and Gideon didn't miss the tiny cringe she tried to hold back. He wasn't sure what that was about. He thought she looked great in her long black skirt and deep purple long-sleeved shirt. And even though her hair, which she'd tucked into a haphazard bun, was a little on the wild side, he appreciated her bohemian look. This was what she'd looked like at home in the apartment they'd shared for a short time. Real. Comfortable. *His.*

The thought came out of nowhere, and regret slammed into him. Miranda Moon had never really been *his.* She was a free spirit who couldn't—shouldn't—be tamed. But there had been a time when she'd offered what she could to him and he'd walked away, knowing that the path he'd chosen wasn't one that would ever work for her. They were just too different. Had different goals. As a couple, they would've never made it. He'd been certain of it then. And judging by the internet search he'd run the night before he was even more certain of it now.

Miranda Moon was a bestselling author of paranormal romance. He was a numbers guy with his father's high-profile media company. He spent his days in meetings and boardrooms. She spent hers in cafes creating her art and traveling to promote her books. It was exactly what he'd always wanted for her. Not to be stuck in LA, with him, and expected to play the supportive wife like his mother had for over twenty years before his dad left her.

"Give me an hour? I've been working all day and wouldn't mind a chance to clean up," she said. "I can meet you somewhere. We could go to Woodlines. Or if you want something more casual, there's a great new pizza place called Mystyk Pizza just down the street."

"Pizza sounds perfect," he said. "But you should know there's no need to clean up. You look great. As always."

A pink flush crept over her cheeks, and he loved that his words had an effect on her. "That's sweet, but I'd feel a lot better after a shower. It's been a long day."

The image of Miranda, naked with water cascading over her body, made every part of him come alive. What he wouldn't do to join her. "Of course. An hour it is then." He stood and held out a hand to her. When she took it, he gently tugged and then led her out of the café. "Which way is your car?"

She laughed. "It's Keating Hollow, Gid, not downtown LA. You don't need to walk me to my car."

He shrugged, unfazed. "It never hurts to be a gentleman."

The sweet smile she flashed him made his insides come alive, and when she gestured to her black Mercedes, he chuckled. It was just the kind of car he'd pictured her driving. She had a very earth-witch style but always had liked her creature comforts. With his hand on the small of her back, he walked with her to the vehicle and then pressed a kiss to her cheek. "See you soon, Miranda Moon."

Gideon didn't miss the way her breath caught or her tiny shiver. And suddenly he was transported back seventeen years to when he first met her and had known instantly that they had a connection. It was still there and just as strong as it had ever been.

Miranda nodded, clicked the lock on her key fob, and slid into the driver's seat of the small car. With a tiny wave, she drove off down the street. Gideon stood on the cobbled sidewalk and watched until her car disappeared into the night.

"You're not lost, are you?" a friendly voice said from behind him.

Gideon turned and jerked back when he recognized Cameron Copeland, a screenwriter who'd penned Ace Media's highest grossing film to date. Gideon laughed and shoved his cold hands into his wool coat. "Nope. I'm here for a much-needed quiet vacation. You?"

Cameron mimicked Gideon and rocked back on his heels. "I was called in to meet with an actor for my next project. Turns out Silas Ansell is spending the holiday season here with his sister. Since I'm here, I decided to hang out and write for a while. Seems like the perfect place to relax and let the words flow."

"Silas Ansell, huh? I hear he's Hollywood's newest darling." Gideon could small talk with the best of them.

"He is. At least he's talented. And I hear he's a total pro on the set. Not that I care much about that. I just want an actor who can bring my work to life on the screen, not make up their own script, if you know what I mean."

Gideon did. Cameron Copeland was the kind of screenwriter who was precious about his work. Any changes or modifications had to be approved by him, per his latest contracts. He'd earned that right, though. The man had three

Oscars to his name and countless other awards. "Is it going well?"

"Sure. The kid wants to work with me, so I think it's a lock." His smirk implied he was taking all the credit for landing the actor with the most buzz at the moment.

Gideon was certain that, if he asked around, everyone from the executive producer right down to the company's unpaid interns would take credit for getting Silas on board, but Gideon didn't care about egos. All he cared about was good films and television. The types of productions that spoke to people in some way. It was interesting that his job required him to care about the numbers and money, but while he did his job to the best of his ability, the truth was he'd only stayed in the business so that he could have some sort of hand in bringing good work to the masses... even if he wasn't the one creating it. "Excellent. Well, I have somewhere to be." He nodded to Cameron as he passed and added, "Good luck."

"Don't need luck when you have hard work on your side," Cameron chirped.

Gideon pretended he didn't hear that last bit. Instead, he hunched his shoulders and headed to the Keating Hollow Inn where he was staying. If Miranda was going to get prettied up, the least he could do was put on a clean pair of jeans.

MYSTYK PIZZA TURNED out to be the kind of place that rippled with magic. The moment Gideon stepped through the door, his body felt alive, energized. Clearly, the place was run by fire witches, and they had played to their strengths. The walls had large burnt-wood art pieces depicting various scenes from Keating Hollow. His favorite was a swimming hole down by the river that appeared to have witches dancing in the moonlight. They just looked so... free. But there were also scenes from Main Street, a local winery, and another one of a small family orchard. It was nice to see the town being documented with someone's art.

After waiting patiently for the hostess, she seated him in a secluded booth in another room in the restaurant and assured him she'd escort his guest to him as soon as she arrived. As he sat and waited, he sipped his wine and stared into the hearth of one of the many fireplaces as the flames flickered and morphed into a variety of holiday-themed scenes: a family building a snowman, Santa and his reindeer flying high over a village, carolers singing around a Christmas tree, witches burning a log for Yule. He was transfixed and a little envious another fire witch had chosen to use their gift in such a way.

What was he using his for? Nothing lately, other than putting out Jax's hair fire. He didn't even have cause to light a fire in his own hearth at home. It was never quite cold enough in southern California to justify one.

"Mr. Alexander?" a woman in jeans and a black button-down shirt asked.

"Yes?"

"Hi. I'm the manager here at Mystyk Pizza. Ms. Moon just called with a message. It appears she's having car trouble and won't be able to make it."

Car trouble? Damn. Standing, he dropped some money on the table and said, "Thank you for the update. I'll be back another time."

"Of course." The manager stepped aside, letting him hurry past her.

Gideon didn't have any idea where Miranda lived or exactly where to look for her, but he did know which direction she'd gone when she'd left an hour ago, and the town just wasn't that big. It wouldn't take much searching to find her.

CHAPTER 5

*M*iranda sat behind the wheel of her car and let out a cry of frustration. What was this? The fourth or fifth date in a row that had gone horribly wrong? Maybe the sixth. How could her recently serviced Mercedes just die without warning?

How many times had she daydreamed about the opportunity to reconnect with Gideon again? More than she could count, and finally, here was her chance. She knew they led very different lives and this dinner date wasn't going to turn into anything more than a friendly reunion. But whatever it was, she was looking forward to spending some time getting to know who he was now versus who he'd been fifteen years ago. She'd been trying to tamp down her nervous energy, but it had only gotten worse the closer she got to Main Street. Then just as she was about to turn right onto the main road, the car had just died and rolled to a stop.

The first thing she did was check the gas gauge. It would be just like her to run out of fuel, especially since she'd been in deadline mode for the past few weeks. But no. The gauge said she still had more than half a tank. And that was where her knowledge of vehicles ended. There was no point in even checking under the hood. She wouldn't know what she was looking at anyway.

After calling for the town tow truck, she swallowed her disappointment and called Mystyk Pizza to have them relay a message to Gideon. If she was honest with herself, she was more upset about missing her date than whatever it was that caused her car to break down. The car could be fixed. But would there be a second, no third, chance with Gideon? Not if he was leaving town soon.

Miranda leaned back against her seat and closed her eyes, trying to block out the fierce disappointment that had settled in her chest.

Tap, tap.

The sound of someone tapping on her window made her let out a startled cry as she nearly jumped right out of her seat. "Holy crow's feet!"

"Miranda? Are you all right?" The muffled voice belonged to none other than Gideon Alexander.

She pushed the door open and stepped out into the cold December air. "Gideon? How did you find me?"

He gave her a self-satisfied smile. "It wasn't that hard. Keating Hollow isn't exactly a bustling metropolis."

Blinking, she stared at him, touched that he'd made the effort to find her. But then she laughed. "Did you show up here to be my knight in shining armor? Because I already called the tow truck guy. He should be here—" She glanced at the time on her phone and frowned. "He was *supposed* to be here ten minutes ago."

"I'll wait with you," he said, wrapping his hand around hers and giving it a squeeze.

Miranda glanced down at their connection as his touch sent flashes of memories of them together through her mind. She'd worked so hard to forget what it was like to be with him, but her body hadn't gotten the message. All she wanted to do was walk into him and let him wrap those strong arms around her. She sucked in a sharp breath and pulled her hand away. She couldn't do this. Couldn't go down this road again. Her heart couldn't take it. "That's nice of you, Gideon, but it's not necessary. I'll be fine. Maybe we can get a raincheck on dinner?"

He took a moment to study her and then slowly shook his head. "No. No raincheck."

"Oh." Her heart sank. It was official; she was cursed. She had to be. Why else had her dating life taken such a wrong turn? "Are you leaving Keating Hollow soon?"

"What? No. Or more accurately, I haven't decided when I'm leaving. When I said no raincheck, I meant that we're not going to let a little car problem ruin the evening. After the tow truck arrives, we'll grab some dinner."

Miranda's phone buzzed, and she glanced at it again, groaning. "He's been called to an emergency on the highway. There's no ETA now. He'll text when he's on his way."

"I guess he's the only tow truck service in town?" Gideon asked.

"Yep. The next closest one is in Eureka. But they'd charge a huge service fee to come all the way out here and get my car. It's better to wait."

Gideon glanced at her car that was safely off to the side of the road. "Come on. The car will be fine here. Let's go get you something to eat. I'll bring you back when he texts you."

Miranda cut her gaze to her car and then back to Gideon. "Are you sure? I don't know how long he's going to be."

His lips twitched into a smile. "I'm more than sure. There's no way I'm leaving you here on the side of the road. So, either we both sit here and wait, or you let me take you to get something to eat. Which will it be?"

Her eyes sparkled, and all the frustration that had been clouding her expression vanished. "Let's eat."

"I'm ready when you are." He waited for her to grab her purse from her car, and after she locked up, he guided her to the passenger side of his SUV.

Once they were both buckled in, she said, "Maybe we should go to my place."

His eyebrows shot up as he looked at her in exaggerated surprise. "Did I hear you correctly? Did Miranda Moon suggest dinner at her house? Are you saying you learned to cook?"

Miranda threw her head back and laughed. It was just like old times, and warmth started to spread from her chest out to her limbs as she relaxed into her seat. "No, actually," she said. "But I do have some leftovers from last night."

"Right. The food you and Jax never got to eat. That will work." He chuckled and started the SUV. "Which way to *chez Moon?*"

Miranda guided him through the short drive to the house at the end of the road that was nestled among the tall redwoods. The house was modest, but it was secluded and quiet. She'd thought that was what she'd need in order to get back into the groove of writing, but it turned out she rarely worked there. Instead, the house had become somewhat of an oasis that recharged her batteries instead.

"This is a great piece of property, Miranda," Gideon said.

She wasn't surprised he liked it. He'd always been a huge fan of nature. If she had to guess, she'd say wherever he lived now wasn't far from the woods. "Thanks. I'm just renting for now until I decide if Keating Hollow is my forever home."

"You don't know if you want to be here permanently?" he asked as he wound his way down her driveway.

"I didn't when I signed the month-to-month lease. But now...?" She shrugged. "I can't really imagine being anywhere else. I'm in no hurry to make any moves."

He glanced over at her. "Waiting for the universe to speak to you?"

"Exactly." Miranda grinned at him. Guh. She'd missed this part of their relationship. There wasn't anyone else in the world who knew her as well as he did. "One day I'll just know, and then I'll either move on or see if the owner of this place is interested in selling."

Gideon stopped the SUV in front of her garage and looked over at the house. Miranda studied it, trying to determine what he saw in the modest cabin. It was cute but small, with an upper and lower wooden porch. The porches had been what she was drawn to. That and the large office on the second floor. But to him, he probably saw a place that needed a lot of TLC and an add-on or two.

"It looks exactly like what I'd picture you living in," Gideon said. "Almost like a fairy or woodland cottage. I bet you feel really peaceful here."

Unexpected tears stung her eyes, but she quickly blinked them back. How could he still be so attuned to her after all this time? "Yeah, I do. This place settles and restores me. It's really something."

"It's something special, Miranda."

She wanted to tell him that *he* was something special, but she bit back the impulse. That kind of talk was totally out of bounds. If she started blurting her feelings out everywhere, that was only going to end up with her heart crushed just like last time. She pasted on a smile and said, "And you haven't even seen the inside yet."

"Knowing you, it's magical." He winked and then hopped out of the vehicle.

Miranda rushed to follow him and took him by the hand to lead him to the front door. Just because she couldn't say how she felt, that didn't mean she couldn't show him. She never had been good at holding back her emotions. Besides, he'd started it with the handholding earlier. To her relief, he wrapped his fingers around hers and held on, letting her tug him up the walk.

Once she got the door open, she flipped a switch near the door, causing the outside of the house, including the porch and about a dozen trees, to light up with hundreds of clear twinkle lights.

"Whoa," he said, scanning the property. "Looks like someone is ready for the holiday."

She nodded. "You have no idea. I've developed a love of all things Christmas. Wait until you see the rest." Miranda flicked another switch, lighting up the inside and the ten-foot Christmas tree that occupied her entire dining room. Since it was just her, she usually ate at the bar in her kitchen.

Immediately upon entering her house, he walked straight toward her tree, touched her favorite glass ornament, and then turned to her with awe in his voice. "You kept it all this time."

"Of course I did." It was the ornament he'd gotten for her during the last Christmas they'd spent together. The entire tree was decorated with nothing but lights and handblown ornaments. After Gideon gave her that first glass ornament, she'd made a point of only buying them from artists. It was something they'd talked about doing when they were together and then she'd followed through, adding a few more each year.

Gideon walked over to her and cupped her cheek. His gaze bored into hers for a few beats before he said, "You're amazing."

Miranda's heart felt as if it was going to burst from pure emotion. She couldn't stop herself from leaning in, needing more from him. But before she could brush her lips over his, he pulled back and cleared his throat.

"So. We should get dinner before your tow truck guy calls," he said, unable to look her in the eye.

"Right." Disappointed, but knowing he'd done the right thing, she retreated to her kitchen and pulled the two containers out of her fridge. In no time, she had the lasagna and seafood risotto reheating in her oven.

CHAPTER 6

*G*ideon poured them both a glass of wine and then followed Miranda into her cozy living room. The heels of her boots clattered on the worn wooden floors, and her lacy black skirt hugged her curves in all the right places. He wouldn't have guessed it to be possible, but she was even more beautiful now than she had been back in college. It wasn't her looks so much as her confidence. She just moved like a woman who was comfortable within her own skin, and damn if that didn't turn him on.

Miranda sat at the far end of a purple velvet couch that was placed in front of a large picture window. Gideon imagined that during the day it must've felt like she was living among the trees, which was likely why the place was so good for rejuvenating her. His own home in Malibu had a view of the ocean, but it wasn't like this. Sure, it was gorgeous, but it didn't have the connection to the earth that this place had. He knew deep down in his soul that Keating Hollow was Miranda Moon's place. Even if she hadn't fully committed yet, this town was destined to be her forever home.

He took a sip of the wine and decided it was time to get to know who Miranda was now and stop crushing on the woman he knew fifteen years ago. "What brought you to Keating Hollow?"

"A book signing." She smiled and her eyes sparkled when she continued. "Yvette Townsend opened up a bookstore completely devoted to paranormal, and when she was still struggling to put the store on the map, she invited a bunch of us to come do a signing. Usually those types of events are fairly low-key, but she went all out on the promotion and the next thing she knew, it was the most popular book signing event this side of the Mississippi. Ever since that first time traveling to Keating Hollow, I knew I wanted to move here. It just calls to me, you know?"

"I can see that." He loved the way her expression was so serene, as if every part of her all the way down to her soul was content.

"What about you? You never did tell me what brought you to Keating Hollow. It's not exactly a hub of industry," she said.

She was smiling when she said the words, but it didn't stop Gideon from wincing internally. He knew she was teasing him, but the innocent jab hit him harder than he'd expected. He hadn't always been all about big business. There was a time in his life when he'd have wanted to live in Keating Hollow just as much as Miranda clearly did. "After all that mess with Silas Ansell went down in the press, one of the travel journalists did a spotlight on Keating Hollow. I happened to see it in a magazine while waiting at the healer's office. And the next thing I knew, I was making a reservation at the Keating Hollow Inn."

"Just like that?" she asked. "This wasn't planned?"

"Just like that," he confirmed, already understanding that the universe had a hand in getting him to Keating Hollow. He didn't know why or what it would mean for the future, but he knew there was a reason he was back here with Miranda Moon. That didn't mean they were destined to get back together. He didn't see how that would work with him in LA and her settled in the redwoods, but something had brought them together and eventually he'd be shown why. "My father wasn't too happy about my sudden departure, but like I told you before, I don't vacation, so he wasn't really in a position to stop me. It's been years since I've taken any real time off."

Her eyes clouded over with something he couldn't quite read, but when she blinked, they were clear again. "It's good you're taking some time for yourself. What do you plan to do while you're here? It's not exactly great weather for hiking, but that's what most people do when they visit the redwoods."

It was on the tip of his tongue to say he was going to spend as much time with her as possible. But he swallowed the impulse. He couldn't say something like that and then walk away from her again. "Relax. Sleep. Do some Christmas shopping." He shrugged. "Maybe I'll even paint a little if there's studio space around here somewhere."

Miranda sat up straight and eyed him with curiosity. "You still paint?"

She'd asked the question as if she couldn't believe that he'd kept up his art even after rejecting a career path as an artist.

"Sure. It takes less space than sculpting, though I do have a sculpting studio at home." What he didn't say was that he hadn't stepped foot into his studio in over five years. He wasn't even sure why he told her about his space. Maybe just to put words to the fact that his art was still important to him even if he hadn't made time to create.

"That's great, Gideon. I'm glad you're still feeding that part of yourself." She smiled brightly at him, making him feel like a fraud.

Gideon cleared his throat and changed the subject. "Tell me about your writing career. How's it going?"

Miranda launched into a monologue of everything she'd written to date, with the exception of the one book he'd actually read. *Witching for You*. He knew she'd written it about them. He also knew his father had tried to stop its publication, but behind the scenes, Gideon had threatened to quit and walk away forever if his dad didn't leave it alone. It was one thing to derail his life for his father. It was entirely another to mess with Miranda's.

When she finally came up for air, she gave him a sheepish grin. "Sorry. I just get so passionate about my writing and the business. I guess I got a little carried away."

"No need to apologize. I enjoyed hearing about your career. I'm glad you're doing well and living the life you always wanted." He reached for her hand again. "It's… inspiring."

Her features softened, and she gazed at him with a tenderness he hadn't seen in forever. It made his heart speed up and his arms ache to hold her. "Gideon, I—"

The timer started to beep, indicating that their dinners were ready to be taken out of the oven.

"Saved by the bell!" she said and jumped up to retreat to the kitchen.

With the spell that had been weaving between them broken, they sat at her kitchen bar, making chit chat about the town and eating until her phone buzzed indicating that the tow truck had finally made it to her car.

True to his promise, Gideon drove her to meet the tow truck driver, where she handed over the keys, signed some paperwork, and instructed him to take it to the dealership in Eureka. It wasn't long before Gideon pulled up in front of her house again.

"I've decided to stay through Christmas," Gideon blurted.

"What?" Miranda turned to him, her forehead wrinkled in confusion. "Aren't you going to spend the holiday with your dad?"

Gideon shook his head, not sure what impulse had made him blurt out his hastily decided plan. "Dad is headed to some tropical beach with wife number four, and my sister is spending the holidays with her in-laws. She invited me of course, but I'd rather recharge here."

"I guess I don't blame you," she said, eyeing him with something that looked an awful lot like mischief. "It's a great place to spend Christmas. There's even a Christmas ball that I'm in charge of planning. If you're interested..." Her voice trailed off as she waited for him to respond.

"Are you asking me on a date, Miranda Moon?" he asked, unable to keep the stupid grin off his face.

"Not exactly," she said with a nervous chuckle. "But if that's part of the deal, who am I to say no?"

He laughed. "Part of what deal?"

"I need some help getting it all together. The type of help

that involves muscle and probably some creativity. Are you game?"

There was no hesitation on his part. She'd just offered him a chance to spend an open-ended amount of time with her. No way was he going to turn that down. "Absolutely. Just tell me where and when, and I'll be there."

"Perfect." She leaned over and pressed a kiss to his cheek. "You're a lifesaver. How about you give me your number and I'll call you with the details?"

"You got it." He handed her his phone and let her add herself as a contact. A moment later, he heard her phone buzz, and he knew she'd texted herself so she'd have his information, too.

"Thanks again, Gideon. It was really nice to catch up," she said, already pushing her door open.

Gideon jumped out and ran over to her side, holding the door as she climbed down to the ground.

"Thanks," she said with a chuckle. "But you didn't need to do that. I'm perfectly capable of getting in and out of your vehicle."

"I know you are," he said, placing his hand on the small of her back and guiding her to her front door. "But then I wouldn't have had an excuse to do this." He slipped his hands around her waist and pulled her in close until their lips were almost touching. "I've missed you, Miranda. More than you know." And then he pulled her all the way to him and kissed her the way he'd been dreaming about ever since he'd walked out of her life all those years ago.

CHAPTER 7

"*Y*our hands are magic," Hope told Esme, the manicurist massaging her hands and forearms.

"You need a full massage," Esme said, digging a thumb into Hope's palm. "That tension you're obviously carrying around in your neck and shoulders is making me wince."

"Do you ever get a turn on the massage table?" Miranda asked from her spot next to Hope. The two of them, along with Shannon and Hanna, were at A Touch of Magic for their manicures and pedicures before they headed out to dinner.

"Rarely," Hope admitted, closing her eyes as Esme pinched the pressure point between her thumb and forefinger.

"She needs it now more than ever," Hanna said, inspecting her freshly painted red nails. "I don't know how she does it with all that family drama. I'd be ready to scream by now."

"Family drama?" Shannon asked. "What the heck

happened? I thought the Townsends never had family drama."

The Townsends were practically the heartbeat of Keating Hollow. Lin Townsend owned the town brewery while his daughters owned the inn, the spa, and the bookstore. Hope, who wasn't Lin Townsend's daughter, worked at the spa with her half-sister Faith. Miranda, who'd heard the stories, chuckled, "I wouldn't say never any drama. A half-sister did show up out of the blue this year."

Hope laughed, and some of her pent-up tension seemed to roll off her shoulders. "That's true. Only I had no idea I was related to any of them. As usual, this drama revolves around Gia." She turned to Miranda to clarify. "That's the name our mother uses, otherwise known as Gabrielle Townsend. Anyway, now that the holidays are here, she's desperately trying to get us to commit to a family gathering. But Noel and Faith aren't talking to her at all, and Abby and Yvette, while they are wary, want to try. I'm mostly with Noel and Faith on this one, but Lin is pushing us to give her a chance."

"Really?" Shannon asked. "I can't imagine him having any goodwill toward his ex-wife, considering she abandoned everyone to live the life of a potions addict."

Hanna stood and moved to one of the massage chairs while she waited for her pedicure. "Lin just wants everyone to heal. He doesn't think that's going to happen as long as his girls are shutting Gia out. But I don't know. Gia is a mess, and if it were me I wouldn't want to spend a strained holiday with her either."

Miranda chewed on her bottom lip. She didn't have any family left. Her parents had been older when she was born and had passed on almost a decade ago, leaving her with a modest but not insignificant inheritance. It was all she had left of them, and she'd have gladly given it all back if she had a chance to see them again. Especially her mother. She couldn't imagine being estranged from her for even one day. Of course, her parents hadn't abandoned her or been potion addicts either. She couldn't say she blamed any of the Townsend sisters for not wanting that in their lives.

"Sorry, Miranda," Hope said, leaning back into her chair. "I'm sure you don't want to listen to my holiday woes. Let's talk about something more exciting. Like your movie! You must be so excited."

Miranda glanced at the pretty woman. Her honey-blond hair was piled on her head in a messy bun, and her big green eyes were wide with interest. "Yeah. I guess I am, though I still haven't been able to get through to my agent, so I only know what Shannon told me."

The other three women all swiveled their heads to look at Shannon. The redhead laughed. "Okay. Hit me. What do you want to know?"

"Who's starring in it besides Silas?" Hanna asked.

"Do we get to go to the premier?" Hope gave her a cheeky grin.

Hanna and Hope fired off a few more questions about where the movie would be filmed and if Shannon would be on set.

"Let's see," Shannon said, tilting her head to the side and eyeing them coyly. "I'm not allowed to say who else is in the film until they announce it. If you guys want to go to the premier, I'm sure Silas can work his magic and get extra tickets. Although, I bet Miranda gets a stash of her own. No, I won't be on set. And I don't know if they've decided where to film it yet. Canada has been a popular location lately. So have New Orleans and Atlanta. I guess we'll find out." Shannon turned her attention to Miranda. "Anything you're dying to know?"

Miranda started to shake her head but then asked, "When does it start filming? Is there a tentative date yet?"

"Early January."

"Whoa. That's fast," Hanna gasped out.

"Yep," Shannon confirmed. "It was supposed to be this summer, but I just got word they moved it up. No idea why. Probably scheduling issues."

Miranda nodded. It was fast. And considering she had consultation rights for the script, she was starting to get uneasy about the lack of communication from her former agent. She was supposed to have the option to read the script and give input.

"Have you talked to your agent yet?" Shannon asked as if she could read Miranda's mind.

Miranda shook her head. "Nope. I called again today, but her assistant just keeps saying she's 'in a meeting.'"

Shannon frowned. "That's not good."

"Tell me about it."

Esme moved on from massaging Hope to working on Miranda's hands. She dug in and then let out a grunt before saying, "Dang, girl. You're just as tense as Hope."

"I'm a writer. I just finished a book yesterday," Miranda said with a contented sigh. "You're really good at this."

"That's good to hear." Esme winked at her and continued to ease the stress from her hands.

"I want to hear about that new hottie in town," Hanna called. "What's his name? Gideon something?"

Shannon chuckled. "Gideon Alexander. He's a bigwig for Ace Media."

"Oh?" Hanna asked. "Is he involved in the movie, too?"

"Nope," Miranda said at the same time Shannon said, "Sort of."

Miranda gave Shannon a look that told her to shut it.

"Oops." Shannon clamped a hand over her mouth. "Sorry."

"Um, what's this about?" Hope asked, leaning forward in her chair with her mouth open. "Is there something going on with you and the hottie movie exec?"

Miranda closed her eyes and sighed. Did she really want to talk about this? Shannon already knew the movie was about her and Gideon. Likely when the movie came out that would become common knowledge at some point. It wouldn't take long for the press to figure it out. She should just tell them. Besides, these people were her friends. They should hear it from her, right? "The book is based on my relationship with Gideon. We dated for a couple of years in college."

"Oh. Em. Gee," Hope gasped out. "Gideon is Greyson?"

"Yep." Miranda sat back in her chair and waited for the inevitable questions.

Her friends did not disappoint. She waited until they got the most frequently asked questions out of the way and then held up her hand for them to stop. "No, I didn't tell Gideon I was writing it. Yes, he knows it's about us. No, I don't know if he's read it, and no, we've never talked about the ending. Anything else?"

Shannon leaned forward and caught Miranda's eye. "There's something still there between the two of you, isn't there?"

Miranda shook her head but felt her cheeks heat with a flush.

"Uh, that blush sure makes it look like something," Hanna said.

Squeezing her eyes shut, Miranda squeaked out, "He kissed me last night, but it's nothing. Really."

"Right. Nothing," Shannon said, sarcasm dripping from her tone.

All three of the other women laughed, and Miranda couldn't help joining in.

"Well, maybe this is the second chance that was meant to happen." Hope grabbed a mimosa off a nearby tray and raised it in a mock salute.

"Maybe." But she couldn't let herself think that way. He was a city guy while she was meant to live in Keating Hollow. The small town was a slice of heaven and the only place that had ever made her feel at peace.

They all drank to second chances, even Miranda, who knew it was a bad idea to wish for the impossible.

An hour later, the foursome strolled into the Townsend Brewery. Christmas lights framed the picture windows while someone had strung the lights on the wall to form the words *Keating Hollow*. The Keating Hollow lights flickered in and out, showing only one letter at a time until they were all lit, and then a tiny Christmas fairy shot out from behind the bar and wrote out *Happy Holidays* in fairy dust.

Miranda let out a giggle as she watched the fairy buzz around drizzling fairy dust on the workers behind the bar and shaking her hips while blowing customers kisses. "Who has the magic to make that happen?" she asked the group.

"Probably Noel," Hanna said, referring to one of Lincoln Townsend's daughters. "She's an air witch."

"It's brilliant," Miranda said, falling even more deeply in love with the town she'd adopted.

"It's fun, that's for sure." Hanna took a seat and draped her wool coat over the back. She was wearing a red dress that showed off her gorgeous dark skin, and she had her curly dark hair tied up into a high ponytail. She was breathtaking, and Miranda made a mental note to use her as inspiration for her next novel.

Miranda sat next to Hanna and ordered a pear cider when the waitress came around. While her friends were chatting about Christmas shopping and holiday parties, Miranda's eye landed on a man sitting by himself at a nearby table. He had his back to her, but when he picked up a book he had lying on the table, she let out a little gasp of surprise.

"What is it?" Hanna asked.

"That guy over there is reading my book." She grinned, never tiring of the thrill when she saw someone with one of her books. "*Witching for You.*"

"Oh, so he likes romance," she said, giving Miranda a wink and a nudge with her elbow.

"Stop." Miranda rolled her eyes. "I have plenty of men readers."

"Really?" Hope said, leaning forward. "Like actual fans that engage with you?"

"Sure. There are many more women, but it's not unusual for men to follow me on social media. I think they like the paranormal aspects."

"That one doesn't have much paranormal though," Hanna pointed out.

"Sure, it does," Miranda said. "The main characters are witches."

"You know what I mean." Hanna nodded to the waitress as she set their drinks on the table. "They have magic, but there are no vampires or werewolves or any evil sorcerers trying to rule the world with their wicked ways."

Shannon laughed. "What are you trying to say? That men don't want to read romance?"

"Well, kinda?" Hanna shrugged. "It just seems like they'd be more into the suspense parts."

"Men read romance," Miranda said, not wanting to get into a discussion about society's rules and expectations about gender. She smirked at her friends and added, "More than you'd think, anyway." Then she got up, effectively ending the thread of conversation. "Excuse me. I'm going to use the restroom."

She made her way across the restaurant and disappeared into the ladies' room. When she was done, she strolled by the guy who was reading her book. She smiled at him, intending to nod and just continue on her way, but he put the book down and said, "Miranda Moon?"

Miranda glanced at her book and then back at the man. Something niggled at the back of her mind. His wide-set dark eyes and salt-and-pepper hair were familiar. Too familiar. She let out a small gasp of surprise. "Cameron Copeland?"

The tall man stood and held out his hand. "It's very nice to finally meet you."

"Um, you too," she said, taking his hand. She wanted to say something interesting or witty, but she was too shocked that the man was reading her book and had recognized her.

"I need to apologize for standing you up the other night. The meeting was very last minute." He waved at the chair opposite him and indicated they should sit. Then he chuckled and raised his hand to his hair. "Though, I haven't heard the end of it from Jax. The guy is losing his mind about his new haircut."

Miranda winced and slid into the chair. Leaning forward, she said, "I feel terrible about that. Does he look okay?"

Cameron let out a snort. "Look okay? You've seen him, right? I'm pretty sure he could wear a bag over his head and the guys would still be hitting him up."

It was Miranda's turn to laugh. "Guys, huh? So not only did you stand me up, but you also sent someone who plays for the other team in your place?"

"At least he was pretty to look at, right?" Cameron winked.

"Fair enough." Miranda sat back and eyed her book that was lying on the table. "Do I dare ask what you think of my work?"

His gaze followed hers. "I'm only halfway through, but so far? It's engaging and full of heart. Exactly the type of story I'd love to put on the big screen."

Miranda shook her head, certain she'd heard incorrectly. "Um, what?"

"I hear they've already hired a screenwriter for the movie," he added. "But what do you think about working together on something else? Could we get together tomorrow night? Chat about some possibilities?"

"Work together on something else?" she stammered, completely stunned. "You mean a script?"

"Sure." He was grinning at her, clearly amused that he'd blown her mind with his offer to collaborate. "We can discuss it tomorrow. What do you say?"

"Yes," she blurted. "Absolutely. Tomorrow is great."

"Good." He slid a business card over to her. "Tomorrow at

seven. How about the Cozy Café? I hear they have great risotto... as long as we stay away from the candles."

With her heart lodged in her throat at the mere possibility of working with him and her face burning from embarrassment, she nodded and forced out, "Sounds perfect."

CHAPTER 8

*P*eople bustled in and out of the Incantation Café while Gideon sat at one of the tables scrolling through his phone to find Miranda's number. They needed to get together to discuss the holiday party she wanted him to help her plan, but the truth was he just *needed* to see her. Ever since he'd kissed her before leaving her at the front door of her cabin two nights before, all he'd wanted to do was head back to her cabin in the woods, curl up next to her, and breathe her in.

The nights they'd spent together all those years ago kept running through his mind, torturing him. He'd spent a great deal of energy putting those memories out of his mind, and all it took was one evening with her for everything to come rushing back. Thinking about walking away from Keating Hollow and resuming his life back in southern California when Christmas was over made his guts churn. But he'd done it once before; he was certain he could do it again.

The phone rang in his ear as he waited for her to answer.

"Hey, you," she said, her voice cheerful. "How has Keating Hollow been treating you?"

"Good." *It would be better if you were with me right now*, he thought as he took a sip of his coffee. "Got dinner plans? I was thinking we could get to work on that Christmas party."

"Um..." She chuckled, and it sounded hesitant, sort of nervous. "Actually, I am busy. Can we do it tomorrow night?"

It was on the tip of his tongue to ask what her plans were, but he swallowed the question. That wasn't his business. "Sure. Tomorrow night. Your place? I'll bring dinner?"

"Sounds perfect." She asked about what he'd been up to since she'd seen him, and instead of telling her the truth, he said he'd been relaxing and exploring the town. "Exploring the town?" she asked with a laugh. "How long did that take? Two hours?"

"Funny. No. More like five." He chuckled. "See why I need you to save me from myself? If you leave me on my own for too long, I'll probably end up getting sloshed at the winery and needing someone to drive me back into town."

"The Pelshes would do that you know. They're good people." She paused, mumbled something to herself, and when she returned to the conversation, said, "I'm sorry. I've got another call. See you tomorrow?"

"Tomorrow it is." He was still smiling when he ended the call. It didn't escape his notice that just the sound of her voice had lit him up, making him feel lighter somehow. After downing the rest of his coffee, he shoved his laptop into his messenger bag and went out to continue exploring the town Miranda loved so much.

Visiting Keating Hollow during the holiday season was magical... literally. All of the shop windows were filled with magical Christmas displays, some with flying reindeer, others with perpetual falling snowflakes, and one even had dancing snowmen. The old-fashioned lampposts were decorated with lights and real blooming poinsettias, and the cobbled sidewalks shimmered with actual sparkling frost, even though the temperatures hadn't yet reached freezing.

There was a lightness to Gideon's step that he didn't usually possess and for once, he found himself looking forward to the festivities of the holiday. How long had it been since he'd taken a moment to really enjoy the wonders of Christmas? Outside of his childhood, he couldn't even remember.

After browsing the bookstore, the chocolate shop, and a gift shop, he made his way into the one art gallery. It was the only store on Main Street that didn't have a magical window display. Instead, there was a painting of a Christmas scene featuring a farmhouse that looked more like a charming village from back east than that of a cabin somewhere near Keating Hollow.

"Good afternoon," a young woman said from behind the desk where she was busy tapping on a keyboard. "Let me know if I can help you with anything or if you have any questions."

"Thanks." Gideon made his way around the store, recognizing many of the artists on display. They were the same ones who were featured in many of the galleries down in Los Angeles. That wasn't at all what he was expecting. He walked over to the desk.

"Did you find anything you like?" she asked, staring up at him hopefully.

"Sure, but nothing that is speaking to me," he said. "I was kind of hoping for something from a local artist. Something made with magic perhaps, or something I couldn't find anywhere else."

The woman frowned slightly. "There is an art fair that runs from spring to fall where the local artisans show their stuff. This gallery has all the top artists around the country."

"I can see that." He pursed his lips. "Well, thank you for your time." Gideon nodded slightly and headed for the door.

Just as he reached for the doorknob, the woman called out, "Hey, do you think that would help?"

He turned around. "Help? You mean with sales?"

She stared down at the counter as she wrapped her arms around herself. "Yeah. Help with sales."

Gideon frowned. There had been a catch in her voice as if she was trying not to cry. He moved back to the counter. "Hey, are you all right?"

She nodded but didn't look up. "I'm sorry. I don't want to keep you."

"You're not keeping me from anything," he said. "You kind of look like you could use someone to talk to."

She looked up and let out a sigh. Her blue eyes were red, but any tears had dried already. "I'm just a little in over my head, I think. This shop was my grandmother's, and she left it to me when she passed. I don't want to close it, but it's barely breaking even, and I can't afford to keep it going when I go back to college this spring. I was thinking if I could improve sales maybe I could hire a manager to run it, but... I dunno. People just don't seem to be buying art."

The art wasn't the problem. Gideon was sure of that. The pieces in the store were high quality and made by successful artists. "I'm not sure that people aren't buying art. If I had to guess, it's more that the people who come here don't want to buy *this type* of art."

She glanced around the shop at the high-end blown glass, hand-painted furniture, wrought iron wall hangings, and various paintings. "What's wrong with this art?"

"Nothing. But people who come to Keating Hollow come here for the magic. They are enchanted by the town. I'm willing to bet they'd buy art that enchants them, too."

"So, you mean art that is made by witches?" she asked, her eyes narrowing as she contemplated what he'd just said.

"Yep. That's what I was looking for. I can get this kind of art back home in any number of galleries. If I'm going to buy something here, I want it to be unique. Something that will remind me of the town." And remind him of Miranda. The thought popped into his head out of nowhere, and he almost groaned. As long as he was in Keating Hollow, she was going to dominate his thoughts. There was no getting around it.

"Huh. Yeah. That makes sense." Her blue eyes started to sparkle as she smiled at him. "You're brilliant." Holding her hand out to him, she said, "I'm Ashe."

He shook her hand and smiled back as he handed her a business card. "It's nice to meet you, Ashe. I'm Gideon. If you get some enchanted art in here, give me a call. I'd love to add something to my collection."

"Count on it." And before he could say another word, she grabbed her smart phone and made a call. "Val? You remember that witch who was making those everlasting snowflakes? Yeah. Do you have her number?"

Gideon nodded his approval and headed for the door. He waved as he left her shop and suddenly had the desire to create. After a quick search on his phone for the nearest art supply store, he hopped into his SUV and headed for Seaside Art Supply over at the coast.

It was dark when he got back to Keating Hollow, and

instead of going out to find food, he placed a call to the Cozy Cave. After stashing his art supplies in his room at the Keating Hollow Inn, he walked over to the restaurant to pick up his dinner. He was waiting at the hostess stand, busy thinking about the piece he wanted to create, when he heard her laugh.

Miranda.

Gideon turned and spotted her at a table with freakin' Cameron Copeland. Their heads were bent close together as they talked and Miranda laughed again, her eyes glinting as she stared at him. Seeing them together, obviously on a date, was like a sucker punch to the gut. He ground his teeth together and had to force himself to stay rooted to the floor. He would not go over and interrupt her again.

"Mr. Alexander? Your order is ready," the hostess said.

He turned to the woman and took the plastic bag she held out to him. "Thanks."

"Have a nice evening," she called after him.

He nodded but knew there wasn't much chance of that. Not now. He wasn't even hungry anymore.

Once he was back in his room at the inn, Gideon put the food into the mini fridge, pulled out a sketch pad, and lost himself in the vision he couldn't get out of his head.

CHAPTER 9

*M*iranda was on cloud nine. Her dinner with Cameron had been everything she could've wished for and more. The two of them had hit it off in a major way. It helped that they were both already fans of each other's work, but when they started brainstorming ideas for a television series set in a small town like Keating Hollow, the outline for a pilot episode came together quickly.

The series would revolve around four brothers who'd inherited a cursed winery. A winery that employed nearly the entire town, and if it went under, it would devastate their beloved community. It was all heart and family and filled with magic. She'd already fallen in love with the lead character, the eldest brother who carried the weight of the world on his shoulders. She couldn't wait to dig into the story arcs for each brother. She'd never worked on a script before, but she was ready to jump in with both feet.

Luckily, Cameron's agent would work the deal for them when it came time to try to pitch it to networks, but she still needed to get in touch with her own former agent to find out about her missing *Witching for You* payments and see about getting a copy of the script for approval. It was just after nine in the morning and the perfect time to try to catch the woman before the day turned too busy. Miranda sat at the bar in her kitchen, took a deep breath, and made the call.

"Olivia Volt's office," the receptionist said.

"Kathy?" Miranda asked. "It's Miranda Moon... again."

"Oh, hi, Miranda," Kathy said, sounding wary. "Olivia's in a meeting. Can she call you back?"

"I don't know. Can she?" Miranda asked and immediately winced. It wasn't Kathy's fault her boss was avoiding her former client.

Kathy gave a nervous chuckle. "You know how it is around here some days. I'm sure she'll call as soon as she can."

"We both know that's not true," Miranda said with a sigh. "Listen, Kathy, I don't even need to talk to Olivia. I just need to know where my check from Witching Hour Productions is for the greenlight of *Witching for You*. Also, I have consultation rights on the script. If you could send it over, I'd appreciate it."

"Um, I'll have to get back to you on those things," Kathy said.

Miranda could hear Kathy tapping away at her keyboard on the other end of the connection. "Will you call me back today either way? I know none of this is on you. I just haven't been able to get answers since Olivia is ignoring me."

"She's not ignoring you," Kathy said, sounding completely unconvincing.

"Right." Miranda actually chuckled. "We both know Olivia and I aren't on great terms anymore. I just want some information without having to get lawyers involved."

It was Kathy's turn to sigh. "Right. I'll see what I can do and for sure will give you a call before I leave the office tonight whether I know anything or not."

"Thank you. I appreciate that." Miranda ended the call, and after pouring herself a second cup of coffee, she sat in her living room and started to outline some notes.

By midafternoon, her brain was mush and Miranda needed some air to clear her head. On a whim, she grabbed her phone and called Gideon.

"Miranda?" he said when he answered. "Is something wrong?"

She laughed. "No. Why did you immediately think something is wrong?"

"I... um," he laughed too. "No one ever calls anymore. It's always texts. The last time someone other than a telemarketer called me it was my dad with bad news about a pet project of mine."

"Pet project? That sounds interesting. Why don't you tell me about it while we take a walk this afternoon?" She asked. "Are you free?"

"Now?"

"Yeah. I've been working all day and need to stretch my legs. I was thinking about a walk down by the river, or we could take a trail through the redwoods. There's one not far from my house. But we'll need to get moving soon; otherwise, we'll lose the light."

"I'll be over in ten minutes," he said.

Happiness bubbled up in Miranda's chest as she set her phone down on her coffee table. How nice was it to be able to just call Gideon up after all these years and invite him out on a whim? It felt right in a way she couldn't quite explain. Then nerves took over as she wondered if she was even presentable. When she was working at home, she often wore pajama pants and old faded T-shirts. Glancing down at herself, she groaned. Not only was she wearing pajama pants, it was a pair that was stained with coffee and something that looked like salsa.

She quickly changed into jeans, a long-sleeved T-shirt, and then pulled on an oversized sweatshirt that said, *I just took a DNA test and it turns out I'm 100% that witch.* After shoving her feet into a pair of running shoes, she did her best to tame her wild brown hair into a thick ponytail before slapping some mascara and lipstick on. She didn't need to be glammed up for a walk, but she didn't want to look like a vampire either.

Just as she was walking back into her living room, a knock sounded on her door. That bubble of happiness returned, and she couldn't help the big smile that claimed her lips when she pulled the door open to find Gideon standing on her front porch. He was also dressed in jeans, but he wore a long-sleeved Henley shirt, and a scarf. He was more *GQ* than *Fitness* magazine, and she had to stop herself from leaning in and kissing his full pink lips.

Gah!

She shook her head, trying to dispel the thought. Gideon had kissed her the other night, and she'd been trying to block it out ever since. If she let herself go back down that road, it would be a disaster when he eventually walked out of her life again.

His gaze traveled down her body and back up again until he was staring her in the eye. "You look great in jeans."

She tsked. "Not as good as when I wear skirts."

He laughed. "I won't argue with that, but I like casual Miranda. Seeing you like this reminds me of simpler times."

Miranda couldn't argue with that. Back in college, life had been simpler. "You look pretty great yourself. Did you just come from a catalog photoshoot or something?"

"Keep saying things like that and my ego is going to be so big I'll be unbearable." He winked. "But no. No photoshoot. I was actually at the inn working on a new project."

Miranda grabbed her waterproof jacket and slipped out the door, gesturing for Gideon to follow her. "New project? I thought you were on vacation. Did your father rope you into developing a new movie?"

He fell into step beside her as they moved toward the back of the cabin. "Nah. It's not for work. This is an art piece. Just something I'm trying out."

Miranda paused and turned to give him her full attention. "An art piece? Are you painting again?"

"No, I was sketching some ideas." He shoved his hands into his pockets. "Enough about that. It's nothing, really. Just a way to relax. Tell me about your upcoming book. What's it about?"

Miranda snorted. "It's a second-chance paranormal romance. He left her to go be the alpha of his pack while she went off and formed her own coven. Now by a quirk of chance, they are living in the same town and obviously can't stay away from each other. The only problem is he's a shifter and supposed to mate with another shifter, and since she's a witch... problems arise."

"Do they get together in the end?" he asked her.

"It's a romance. What do you think?"

Gideon chuckled. "I guess that's fairly obvious. I can't wait to read it."

Miranda stopped in her tracks, her mouth open slightly as she stared at him. "You read my books?"

He blinked at her. "Not all of them, no. But I have read *Witching for You.*"

Her mouth was dry, and her heart was thudding against her breastbone. He couldn't be serious.

Moving in closer, he pressed his palm to her cheek and gazed into her eyes as he added, "It's a beautiful story, Mandy. You have no idea how many times I've imagined what our lives would've been like if we'd gotten the ending you wrote for us."

Tears burned Miranda's eyes, and she had to look away. Otherwise she was going to lose it completely. After taking a few deep breaths, she said, "I didn't write our ending, Gideon. I wrote the beginning we deserved."

"Damn," he said so softly she barely heard him. "I'm so sorry we never got that chance."

She couldn't look at him as she said, "I know. Me, too."

He let out a humorless bark of laughter. "What do you have to be sorry for?"

This time she did look at him when she said, "For being so angry at you when you chose to live a different life than I wanted for you. It wasn't fair. You deserved to follow your dreams just like I did."

Emotion she couldn't quite place flashed in his dark gaze. Regret? Sadness? Unease?

"I'm sorry. I shouldn't have said anything." She pulled back and started to walk again, moving deeper into the grove of trees.

"You don't have anything to be sorry for, Miranda," he said as he quickly caught up to her. "Not then and certainly not now."

"That's kind of you to say." Miranda glanced up, gazing at

the gray sky peeking through the trees. "Let's just put that behind us, okay? We have a Christmas ball to plan."

"As long as we can be friends," he said.

"We're friends. Definitely," she said easily, even though her heart felt like it was breaking all over again. *Son of a shifter*. They hadn't been a couple for over a decade. The feelings shouldn't have come roaring back so fast, and her heart certainly shouldn't be so fragile.

"I mean friends even after I leave Keating Hollow," he said softly, taking her hand in his. "I don't want us to lose touch again."

Miranda internally groaned. How was she going to be "just friends" with the love of her life? "Sure, Gideon. You have my number."

He squeezed her fingers and said, "Good. I'd really like that."

"So, tell me about this pet project your dad killed," she said.

"How do you know he killed it?" Gideon asked, sounding amused.

She rolled her eyes. Gideon's dad wasn't the type of man to do anything he could pawn off on an assistant. "Come on. Why else would he have called you personally?"

"Fair enough." He gazed over at the trickling stream and said, "I actually wrote a treatment for a television pilot. It was about a group of artists just out of college, trying to figure out how to make a living in the internet age."

"That sounds cool. What happened?" she asked.

He shrugged. "He doesn't think it's the right timing. But really, he probably just doesn't think it's good enough. Maybe he's right. I'm not exactly experienced with storytelling."

Miranda knew that wasn't true. In their college days, she'd run a bunch of story ideas by him and he'd always been insightful. She'd always thought of him as a natural storyteller. It was probably why most of the movies he had a hand in producing were critically acclaimed even if they weren't runaway box office hits. "I'd be happy to take a look if you want."

He glanced over at her, his expression unreadable. Then he said, "Maybe. I'm not sure it's worth your time."

"That's for me to decide, don't you think?" she said gently, knowing just how hard it was to show other people your work when you were so close to it.

He nodded but then fell silent.

At one time in their lives, the quiet moments between them were comforting. Now? It was awkward.

Miranda opened her mouth to say something, say anything, when she heard someone talking just ahead of them on the trail. She glanced over at Gideon, noting he was peering up the trail as well.

"I don't know how that's going to work if you're not here," the person said. His voice was familiar, but Miranda couldn't place it right away.

"You know I'm always going to come back here, right?"

Miranda slowed her pace, not wanting to interrupt, but she was too late. They'd just rounded a large tree and found Silas Ansell and Levi Kelley sitting on a fallen log. Silas was staring at Levi, while Levi was staring up into the trees.

"Silas! Levi! Hey there, you two," Miranda said and pasted on a smile. It was clear they'd unintentionally stumbled upon them in the middle of a disagreement. But she didn't want to make it any more awkward for the two teenagers and figured it was best to pretend they hadn't heard anything. "It appears we all had the same great idea. It's lovely out today, isn't it?"

"Hey Miranda," Levi said, springing up as if surprised.

Miranda studied him for a moment. Hadn't he known that they were nearby? He was a spirit witch and could sense people before he saw them. But it appeared his gift had failed him. "Didn't mean to startle you."

He ran a hand through his dark curly hair and let out a nervous chuckle. "I guess I was too distracted."

"It happens to the best of us." She glanced over at Silas and winked.

Silas got up and gave her a hug. "It's good to see you again, Miranda. I've been meaning to give you a call about *Witching for You.*"

When Silas pulled back, Miranda gripped his hands and said, "I heard you got the part of Charlie. Congratulations!"

"Thanks. I'm glad we ran into you. There's actually something about Charlie I wanted to ask you about."

"Sure." A strange combination of heavy sadness and pure joy rippled through her just as it always did when she thought about Cory, aka Charlie. He'd been killed seven years ago by a drunk driver, and the pain was still fresh. But he had also been her favorite person on earth, so thinking about him brought back tons of happy memories, too.

The tall, dark-haired actor tugged her over to the log where he and Levi had been sitting and gestured for her to take a seat. While they both sat, Gideon introduced himself to Levi and the pair started to talk about Levi's favorite hiking spots around Keating Hollow.

"I have a few questions," Silas said to Miranda. "I read the script a few days ago, and if I'm recalling correctly, Charlie's character doesn't really line up with the book version. And I was wondering if you—"

"The script version of Charlie doesn't match the book version?" she asked as one hand flew to her stomach as if she could do anything to soothe the sudden ache. If anyone deserved to be immortalized on the big screen, it was Cory. He'd been a lovely, talented man with an enormous heart.

Silas frowned. "You didn't know?"

Miranda shook her head. "I haven't gotten the script yet. My former agent and I are having trouble connecting."

"Oh." Silas grimaced. "Damn. Then I'm guessing that means you didn't sign off on this."

"Nope. I'm supposed to have consultation rights, too."

Silas sighed. "You're not going to like this."

"Just tell me. What did they do to Charlie?" Trepidation rippled through her, causing her to go completely still.

"They made him closeted until the very end of the story," Silas said.

Miranda considered that. In the book, Charlie had come out to Mandy their freshman year in college. If he was closeted, that would change his story quite a bit, but for a movie it might be workable. "I'd have to read it to see how the writer handled that, I guess."

"There's more." Silas glanced at Gideon quickly and then back at Miranda. "They made it a love triangle between Mandy, Charlie, and Greyson."

Miranda stared at Silas, not quite processing what he'd just said. "Wait. What?"

"Charlie doesn't come out to anyone, not even Mandy, until the very end of the script right before they're supposed to get married."

"Married?" Miranda jumped up and started to pace. Then

she stopped and stared wide-eyed at Silas. "What the hell did they do to my book?"

"I'm so sorry, Miranda. I agreed to the project based on the book. I didn't get the script until after the contracts were signed." He gave her a small smile. "I read it earlier this year after Shannon said you'd moved to Keating Hollow. I loved it."

That was nice of him to say, but she couldn't get over the changes they'd introduced into the script. The love triangle was completely unnecessary, not to mention complete erasure of the character she'd created based on Cory. "I need to see this script. Do you think I could take a look at your copy?"

"Of course." Silas gestured to Levi and Gideon. "Change of plans. We're headed back to my place so Miranda can get a look at the script."

Gideon raised an eyebrow at Miranda in question. "Is everything okay?"

Miranda shook her head. "No. Not okay at all. They've made Charlie one of Mandy's love interests."

"What?" Gideon asked, looking just as confused as Miranda felt.

"Exactly."

CHAPTER 10

$\mathcal{G}$ ideon followed Levi, Silas, and Miranda up the walk to a pristine white cottage. The grounds were rich with lush gardens and Gideon wouldn't have been surprised to see the home on the cover of a magazine.

"Great house," Gideon said. "A little on the smaller side for a Hollywood star, though." He grinned at Silas, teasing him. "Nice to see it hasn't gone to your head yet."

"Oh, it's gone to his head," Levi countered as he rolled his eyes and walked through the living room to the kitchen. "He's already talking about building a house over on the hill near Brian's place."

"This is my sister's house," Silas explained. "You'd think my boyfriend would be happy about the fact that I want my own permanent home in Keating Hollow."

Gideon glanced between the two teenagers. They were glaring at each other, and he got the impression that whatever fight they were having didn't have anything to do with a house.

Levi ignored the jab and started prepping a pot of coffee,

moving around as if he spent a lot of time at the Ansell residence.

Silas sucked in a breath and then moved to the table and picked up a bound set of papers. "Miranda, here you go. Do you want to sit at the table or—"

"I'll take this into the living room if that's okay," she said. "I'd rather get comfortable on the couch."

"Sure. I'll bring you a cup of coffee when it's ready," Silas said.

"Thanks." She turned and headed into the other room, already opening the script.

"Gideon," Silas said. "Can I get you anything?"

"Just coffee when it's ready," he said, taking a seat at the table. He didn't want to bother Miranda while she read the script.

Silas nodded and moved to stand next to Levi, who was staring out the window. They bent their heads together and spoke softly. Gideon busied himself with the Keating Hollow Gazette that was lying on the table. The small publication had a write-up on the holiday town of Christmas Grove, a profile on an author named Georgia Exler who'd recently appeared at the bookstore for a signing, and a news article about the expansion of the Townsend Brewery as they planned to move into producing hard ciders.

But it was the arts market schedule that caught his eye. The event was for local artisans only and was held every Saturday at the town park right up until Christmas Eve. He was looking forward to checking out the creations by the witches of Keating Hollow.

"I'm sorry," Silas said to Levi, catching Gideon's attention.

"I know." Levi leaned over and kissed his boyfriend on the cheek, giving him a small smile. "So am I."

Silas draped an arm over Levi's shoulders and pulled him in for a sideways hug and then took a mug of coffee into the other room.

Levi picked up two mugs and moved to sit across from Gideon, handing him one of the coffees. "Sorry about that. We've been... having a disagreement."

Gideon took a sip of the coffee. "Want to talk about it?"

Levi averted his dark eyes and shook his head.

"I understand. Sometimes a man just needs to process stuff on his own."

"Or maybe his boyfriend should just keep his word for once," Levi blurted. Then he grimaced. "Sorry. I shouldn't have said that."

Gideon set his mug down on the table and took a guess at the problem. "Scheduling issues?"

Levi glanced over his shoulder toward the living room and then back at Gideon. "How did you know that?"

Gideon let out a humorless chuckle. "I've worked in the film industry my entire adult life. I also know that Silas just signed on to an accelerated project. It wasn't that hard to figure out. I imagine the studio is putting a lot of demands on him."

"So, I'm overreacting then?" Levi asked, looking genuinely upset.

"I didn't say that." Gideon was well aware of how hard Hollywood was on relationships. It didn't help that Levi and Silas were both young. The chances of a long-term relationship were slim under the best circumstances. Add in a high-profile acting career and it was a recipe for disaster. Still, the two seemed to care for each other, and if anyone knew what it was like to find their person at a young age, it was Gideon. He'd also let her go, and it had nearly broken him, but it had been right for her. "Your feelings are valid and important."

Levi rolled his eyes. "You sound like my sister Hope."

Gideon's lips twitched with amusement. "Your sister sounds like a smart cookie."

He shrugged. "I guess, but telling me I'm entitled to my feelings doesn't change the fact that Silas is leaving two weeks earlier than he was supposed to and breaking his promise to be here on New Year's Eve. We were supposed to spend it together, just the two of us. I planned—never mind. It doesn't matter what I planned. It just sucks that he won't be here."

"Is he leaving because of filming?" Gideon asked.

Levi nodded. "And that's why I'm not allowed to be upset." He closed his eyes and shook his head. "It's just hard having a long-distance relationship, especially with someone who's always being pulled in twelve different directions. He's been back in town for a week and today was the first day we've had together that didn't involve conference calls or last-minute meetings, and we spent it fighting over when he's leaving."

"That's tough." Gideon gave him a sympathetic smile. "It's not easy letting someone go when we love them so much."

Levi sighed. "Yeah. It's really hard."

"Can I give you some advice?"

"Sure." Levi held Gideon's gaze.

Gideon had to give the kid credit. He appeared wiser than his years, and it was obvious he really cared about Silas the person, not Silas the famous actor. "The hardest thing you can do when you love someone is let them go. But if you love them, you want them to follow their passion, otherwise you're stifling the person you care about most. And that never works."

"If you love someone, let them go?" he asked.

"Exactly."

Levi glanced back at the living room and then back at Gideon, his eyes narrowed in concentration. "How did that work out for you?"

Gideon stared at the young man across from him and then shook his head as he stifled a humorless laugh. "To be honest, Levi. Not well. But she's turned out to be the person she was meant to be, and that's all I've ever wanted for her."

"And what about you?" Levi asked. "Did you turn out to be the man you were supposed to be?"

"Yes," he answered honestly. What he didn't say was that he didn't turn out to be the man he *wanted* to be. He'd been born into the role he played as a Hollywood producer, and he'd done it well. That idealistic artist of his youth had disappeared somewhere along the way, and most days he barely remembered that kid. But walking into Keating Hollow and spending time with Miranda had rekindled something in him, and he was starting to wonder what his life would be like when he went back to LA. Would he slip back into his role as producer, or would he finally find himself making use of his home art studio? He didn't know, and as long as he was in Keating Hollow he didn't need to find out.

"Excuse me for being blunt, but your energy says you aren't exactly happy about that, Gideon," Levi said.

"You can feel my energy?" Gideon felt weirdly exposed, but for some reason, he didn't seem to mind.

"Yeah. Sorry about the intrusion. I'm a spirit witch. It's not something I can control most of the time."

"It's all right." Gideon leaned back in the chair. "It's not exactly a secret that Miranda and I had something special. That book she wrote, it's more fact than fiction. Anyone would regret losing a relationship like that. But life happens. All you can do is keep moving forward."

"That sounds pretty pessimistic to me." Levi leaned forward and lowered his voice. "It seems to me that it's not too late to change things."

"I doubt that's in the cards." Especially since Miranda appeared to be dating Cameron Copeland. There was no doubt she had a lot more in common with the screenwriter than him. Certainly, their lives would be more compatible. Still, the very idea of never having another chance with Miranda made everything inside of him turn to ice. He got up and said, "Excuse me. I think I need some air."

Just as Gideon reached for the backdoor latch, a cry of frustration came from the living room.

"Miranda?" He spun around and rushed into the other room. Silas was nowhere to be found while Miranda was standing in the middle of the room, one fist clutching the script and the other buried in her thick hair as if she were trying to pull her own hair out. "It's that bad?"

Her fierce gaze met his, and she ground out, "They have Mandy hooking up with Charlie and Greyson walking in on them." There were angry tears in her eyes as she added, "This is... It's a garbage rewrite. I need to talk to Olivia right now."

Gideon walked over to her, gently took the script out of her hands, and then pulled her in for a tight hug.

"How could they do this to my book?" she asked him, her voice shaky.

Gideon couldn't say he was completely surprised. Hollywood screenwriters often took source material and completely twisted it into whatever they thought would play better with the audience. Or their egos were so big that they just had to make sweeping changes, otherwise they felt they hadn't put their mark on the work. Sometimes the changes were needed. Sometimes they were necessary. But in the case of *Witching for You*, the rewrites were completely lazy and reeked of clichés. "I'm sorry, Miranda. I'll do anything I can to help you fight this."

She pulled away, shaking her head. "I just need to talk to my damned agent." After yanking her phone out of her pocket and nearly dropping it, she wiped the tears from her eyes and made the call. Her angry expression turned to downright fury as her jaw tensed and her lips twisted into a snarl. "Olivia, you need to call me back immediately. This script is completely unacceptable. If I don't hear from you this afternoon, you can expect to be hearing from my lawyer."

Gideon opened the script and started to scan while Miranda paced the living room, grumbling at her phone. From what he saw, it was even worse than he'd feared. The screenwriter had been heavy-handed with every plot point, and all of the charm of Miranda's novel was completely lost. If he was the producer, he'd have rejected it just on quality alone.

He immediately started to run through the names of the execs who might be working on the project, and he wondered if there was someone he could talk to behind the scenes to get the inside scoop on what exactly was going on. Witching Hour Productions was usually a great studio to work with. Something about this just smelled bad.

"She's not going to call me back," Miranda said. "Now that I've threatened a lawyer, that's how she'll respond. And I don't even *have* a lawyer." She flopped down onto the couch, appearing completely defeated.

"I can get Shannon. She can probably help," Silas said from the doorway between the kitchen and living room. "She has connections. Access to entertainment lawyers."

"I don't want to bother her at the shop," Miranda said.

Silas's face flushed red as he cleared his throat. "I, uh, already messaged her. She's on her way here. Miss Maple is at the store today."

Miranda closed her eyes and said, "All right. I can use all the help I can get."

"I'll be right back," Gideon said and slipped outside. After scrolling through his contacts, he landed on Vincent and made the call.

"Gideon Alexander," his friend Vincent said, sounding both happy and surprised. "Where the hell have you been?"

"Why? Who's looking for me?" Gideon responded as his lips twitched into a smile. Vincent was a good guy who'd worked for him for a few years before he'd been wooed away by a startup. The startup had been acquired by Witching Hour eight months ago, and by some miracle, Vincent had survived the layoffs.

"Lenora for one. Damon for another." He cleared his throat. "I don't know what's going on over there at Ace Media, but there's a ton of gossip about your dad backing this new movie."

"What new movie?" Gideon's brow furrowed. All of their current projects had been on the schedule for months. They weren't supposed to be looking at anything new until January.

"*Witching for You.* You know, that one that's based on the book your ex wrote."

Gideon was stunned into silence. Had he heard Vincent correctly? He couldn't have. "Uh, Vincent, what are you talking about? Why would my father be backing anything at Witching Hour Productions?"

Vincent chuckled. "That's the million-dollar question, isn't it?"

"Oh, hell. I've got to go. Can I call you later tonight?"

"Don't bother. I'm off to Belize with the girlfriend for the holidays. Hold on." There were muffled voices in the background. "Sorry, Gideon. Got to go. Talk to you after New Year's?"

"You got it. And Vincent?"

"Yeah?" he said.

"Thanks, man."

"Anytime."

A moment later, the phone was ringing as Gideon called Lenora, his assistant.

"Finally!" Lenora's voice boomed over the phone. "I can't believe you didn't take any of my calls. What's that about? Did I piss you off or something?"

"No. Calm down," he said, amused by her anger. Lenora had worked for him for ten years and was the one person who was never afraid to tell him exactly what she thought. "I was just trying to take a much-needed break. And if I answered your calls, I'd be pulled back into whatever the crisis of the week is, and we both know you're more than capable of handling whatever it is."

She scoffed. "Not this time. Who's the one person who never listens?"

Gideon groaned. "What's he done this time?"

"He's been locked in his office, taking secret meetings with someone from Witching Hour. At first, I thought there was some sort of merger going on. But when I started badgering his assistant, Kim said he's just financing that movie that's based on you and your ex. She says it doesn't have anything to do with Ace."

"You mean he's *personally* financing it?" Gideon asked, completely confused. His father had tried to stop the book's publication. Now he was backing the movie? That didn't make any sense.

"Yes," Lenora said. "But that's not even the weirdest part."

"It's not?" What could be stranger than his father backing a movie with another media company? And on top of that, the movie was Gideon's story. The story his father had never wanted to see the light of day.

"No. The weirdest part is that he's having his calls bypass Kim. She hasn't answered a call all week. The only reason she knew about him financing it is because her cousin works for Witching Hour and let it slip by accident."

"So he's secretly financing *Witching for You* and doesn't want anyone to know?"

"Exactly," Lenora said. "I tried to tell you days ago, but you never answered."

"Damn. Thanks, Lenora. I appreciate the information."

"You're welcome, but don't freeze me out, all right?" she said with a sigh. "If you don't want me to bother you with anything other than pure emergencies, I can do that. Just say so."

Guilt crawled up his spine. Lenora was an excellent assistant. He should've known she'd understand his need for a break. And if he'd answered her calls, he would've known about his father's strange action days ago. Not that he knew what to do with the information. As far as he knew, his father had never personally backed anything.

Why would he when he had Ace Media? "You got it. I promise to answer and return your calls as long as you don't call me for anything you or someone else in the office can handle."

"I'm on it, boss." She ended the call without saying goodbye, making him grin. Lenora was a no-nonsense assistant and wasting time wasn't in her DNA.

He hit his dad's number and waited. Sure enough, he answered it himself, proving Lenora's intel that his dad was taking his own calls. Gideon couldn't remember a time that Kim hadn't fielded his calls to his father.

"Gideon. Where are you? You're supposed to be back already," his father groused.

"I'm in Keating Hollow, on vacation, right where I told you I'd be."

"Right. Right. Okay then. When are you coming back?"

"Not until after Christmas," Gideon said, frowning. His father sounded distracted, not at all like the high-powered executive who never had time for small talk.

"I guess that's fine. Your stepmother and I will be in Costa Rica until after New Year's. Lenora and Damon can cover for you while you recharge."

Recharge? His father didn't believe in recharging. He lived by the philosophy of work hard and play hard. His idea of recharging was hiring a massage therapist to visit the office on his lunch break. "Good, because I told Lenora not to call unless absolutely necessary."

"Good. That's good."

"What the hell is going on?" Gideon demanded, unable to keep his cool. "Why are you financing *Witching for You?*"

Throm Alexander sputtered, actually *sputtered*, and then cleared his throat. "Where did you hear that?"

"Does it matter?" Gideon ground his teeth together and waited.

"I guess not." There was silence over the line until his father finally said, "I was looking for a decent personal investment, and a friend of mine over at Witching Hour mentioned it. Is that a problem for you?"

"No," Gideon said, caught off guard that his father had thought to even ask him how he felt about it. "But I am surprised. You never wanted Miranda's book published in the first place."

"Can't I do something nice for my son without suspicion?" Throm sounded annoyed now.

There was no way Throm Alexander invested in Miranda's movie just to be nice. Gideon's father didn't do anything without a return. "Cut the crap, Dad, and tell me the real reason."

"I have no idea what you're talking about, Gideon. Now I'm ending this conversation before we both say something we'll regret. Enjoy your holiday. I'll see you in the New Year."

"Da—" The phone clicked, indicating his father had hung up. After trying two more times to reach him and being sent straight to voicemail, Gideon blew out a frustrated breath and walked back into the house.

CHAPTER 11

*M*iranda felt sick to her stomach. She'd just finished reading the script for the second time when Shannon Ansell strode through her front door with her phone pressed to her ear and her jaw clenched in annoyance.

"I don't care if he is busy, Poppy," she said. "I need to talk to Tim immediately. It's important." Shannon nodded at Miranda and then Silas before turning her attention back to her phone call. "We have a breach of contract, and it's time sensitive. No, it's not for Silas. It's my new client, Miranda Moon."

New client? Shannon was taking liberties with the truth, but if it helped get her on an entertainment lawyer's radar, Miranda didn't care one bit.

"Yes. You can call me back at this number. Miranda is here now." She nodded as if Poppy could actually see her. "That's right. We'll be waiting."

Shannon ended the call and turned to Miranda. "Poppy is going to get Tim to call us back as soon as he's out of his meeting." She grabbed Miranda's hands and held them tightly. "How are you doing? Are you all right?"

"No. Not at all." She launched into a rant about the script, her payments, and how she was sure she'd burned the last bridge with her former agent, Olivia Volt. "I feel like I'm out to sea without a paddle."

"Well, your life preserver is here," Shannon said, moving to the couch and pulling Miranda down to sit with her. "If you want me, that is."

Miranda didn't really know any of the specifics regarding Shannon's work managing Silas's career. But it was no secret that Silas was happier than ever with his sister at the reins. And judging by the way she'd handled the call with the lawyer's assistant, Miranda had no trouble believing Shannon was more than capable. "Are you saying you want to manage my film rights?"

"I will if you want me to," Shannon said. "But right now, I'm doing this as a favor. The lawyer, if you end up using him, will have his own fees."

"He's really good. Straightforward guy. I like him," Silas added from across the room. He and Levi were hovering near the entrance to the kitchen.

"I agree," Shannon said. "He's a no-nonsense guy. Tells us like it is, and when the other party is in the wrong, he's a bulldog. But if he thinks things aren't likely to go our way, he tells us that, too, and lets us make the decisions."

"Okay." Miranda glanced at Gideon. His eyes were hooded, and he had a surly expression on his face. She'd watched him pace back and forth when he'd been outside talking on the phone. He hadn't said anything since he'd come back inside though, and she couldn't help but wonder who he'd been talking to. With his connections, it could've

ESSENCE OF THE WITCH

been anyone. Surely if it had been about her movie, he'd have said something, right? "Do you know Tim?"

"Timothy Lufti," Shannon supplied.

Gideon shook his head and said, "No. Never met him, but he does have a good reputation around town."

"Okay. Let's see what he says." Miranda sat back against the couch cushions and draped an arm over her eyes. "I can't believe this is turning out this way. When I sold the movie rights, I honestly never thought the project would get made. Who would've thought they'd butcher it so much?"

"I'm sorry, hon," Shannon said. "It happens way too often when the source material is from a book. Sometimes I'm convinced the screenwriter didn't even read the manuscript."

Miranda groaned. "Not helping."

Shannon patted her leg. "We'll put Tim on it and go from there." Her phone buzzed, and Shannon answered it immediately. She spoke with Tim for a few minutes, and when she ended the call, she turned to Miranda. "Here's what we need to do. We need to send Tim your contract with Witching Hour and your contract with your former agent. He wants to go over both before he gives any advice."

"All right." Miranda stood. "I have both in my files at home. I'll email you copies of them in about an hour."

Shannon got to her feet and hugged Miranda. "I'll do everything I can."

"I know you will. Thank you." She glanced around for Gideon and raised her eyebrows. "Are you coming with me?"

"Yes." He strode over, took her hand in his, and then guided her out of the house. It didn't take long for them to walk to Miranda's house. She was just about to invite him in, when he said, "I've got to go take care of something. Can we take a raincheck on the Christmas party planning?"

"Sure. I guess so."

"Thanks," Gideon ran a hand through his hair. "Call me when you hear back from the lawyer?"

"Um, okay." She narrowed her eyes at him. "What's up with you? You're acting weird."

He let out a surprised bark of laughter. "Me? Weird?"

"Yeah. Totally weird. You haven't said anything since we left Shannon's house, and now you're running off to do some mysterious errand. The Gideon I know would be sticking around to find out what the lawyer says."

"Do you want me to stay?" he asked, his expression suddenly concerned instead of distracted.

"No." She refrained from rolling her eyes and wrapped her arms around herself as a gust of breeze left her chilled. "I can handle this. I just thought... never mind what I thought. I can't do this right now. I'll talk to you later, okay?" She turned and started to enter her front door.

"Miranda," he said softly and gently wrapped his hand around her wrist. "Wait."

She paused but didn't look back at him. Miranda knew what was really bothering her; she just hadn't wanted to say anything about it. Now she couldn't hold it in. "I know you called someone earlier. Was it about *Witching for You?*"

"Yes."

She slowly turned around to face him. "And?"

"I didn't find out anything useful yet," he said. "I want to see if I can find out who's in charge of this project over there and see if I can get someone on the phone to find out why they took such a sharp left turn."

Miranda didn't miss the fact that, instead of looking her in the eye, Gideon was staring over her shoulder into her cabin. Her spine tingled with unease, giving her the sinking feeling that he was holding something back from her. But what could she do other than wait him out? "Fine. But I don't want you fighting this battle for me, Gideon. If there's someone to talk to over there, let my lawyer handle it."

His gaze shifted to hers and softened. "Are you sure? I do have some sway in the industry."

"I'm positive." Her story meant everything to her, but she'd be damned if she let the man who walked away from her all those years ago fight her battles. She could take care of herself. She just needed to know who she was fighting.

"Okay," he said, pushing a lock of her dark hair from her eyes. His touch was light as a feather but also sent electric shocks all over her skin as he brushed his thumb over her cheek. "I won't step in where I don't belong."

Her entire body shuddered slightly as she breathed, "Thank you."

IT WAS early evening when Miranda's phone rang. The number indicated it was from Los Angeles, and she blew out a sigh of relief. She'd done nothing but pace her small cabin ever since she'd emailed her contracts to Shannon.

"Hello?" she said into the phone.

"Miranda Moon? It's Timothy Lufti, the entertainment lawyer who works with Shannon Ansell."

"Yes, I know who you are. Thank you for taking time today to talk with me. Did you get a chance to read through my contracts?"

"I did. First things first. Shannon was able to contact the studio and found out they sent a check to your agent seven weeks ago. That means, according to your agency contract,

DEANNA CHASE

that your agent is in breach. I already have my assistant working on a demand letter for immediate payment. I will also forward a request from you to the studio that all future payments be split. The media company will pay you directly and send your agent her share, so you won't have to deal with her again. Does that sound agreeable?"

"Yes. I didn't know that could be done," Miranda said, feeling a tiny bit of relief. At least she'd get paid. It was something. "What about my consultation rights? Nobody sent me the script, but Silas let me take a look at his copy. I'm supposed to give my input before this thing begins filming."

Tim cleared his throat. "This is where it gets tricky."

Miranda's heart sank. "Okay. Just lay it on me."

"Consultation rights in this context only mean that you must be given the opportunity to have input on the script. It does not mean your notes have to be used. So, while we can and will push the issue, the chances of them making changes, or at least any significant changes, are minimal. And your legal recourse is dubious."

"Why is it dubious?" Miranda asked, closing her eyes and trying not to scream. She shouldn't have been surprised. In fact, while he was explaining that the writer didn't have to use her notes, a conversation with her old agent while they'd been discussing the terms of her contract came rushing back. Olivia had warned her that she likely wouldn't have much say in the final outcome of the movie despite her consultation rights clause.

"If you were to sue them, it would cost a lot. And as long as they let you turn in your notes, it's probable that you'd lose the suit," he said.

Miranda sank into her couch, her chest aching with defeat. "So, I can't do anything at all?"

"I didn't say that. We can press them to let you discuss the changes with them. You never know how that will shake out."

"All right. I'll work on my notes so I'm ready." Her tone was defeated even to her own ears.

"I'll have my assistant keep you and Shannon updated with our progress."

"Thanks, Tim."

"You're welcome. And Miranda?" he added.

"Yeah?"

"Don't hesitate to call if you need anything else."

That surprised her. She didn't know why. He was a lawyer and was likely paid by the minute. But still, after being frozen out by Olivia, having someone who was willing to work for her was refreshing. "I will. Thank you so much. I appreciate your help and your candor."

"That's what I'm here for."

After Tim ended the call, Miranda dropped her phone onto a side table and leaned forward, resting her aching head in her hands. She wasn't sure when the headache had started, but it was bad enough that she knew the only thing left to do was to head to bed and sleep it off.

CHAPTER 12

*G*ideon shoved his hands in his pockets and quickened his pace. After exhausting his contacts with Witching Hour Productions and coming up completely empty, he'd put his phone into his pocket and headed out to walk off some tension.

Something was seriously off. He'd spent the previous afternoon and most of the morning trying to get someone, anyone, from Witching Hour to talk to him about the production of *Witching for You*. Everyone he'd called was either already out of town for the holidays or was tight-lipped. No one was willing to give him the details of which executive was producing the project. They hadn't even been willing to tell him who they'd tapped to direct the film. The one piece of information he'd gotten was about the screenwriter. And the guy, Troy Bix, was a total newbie who'd worked as an assistant writer on one of Ace Media's movies last year.

He'd been itching to call Troy, but out of respect for Miranda, he refrained. To say he was frustrated was an understatement. Gideon Alexander was a man who got things done. He had connections and friends in the industry. The fact that he was being iced out told him one thing; someone was making sure Gideon stayed in the dark. And he was pretty certain he knew exactly who'd given that order.

Throm Alexander had some serious explaining to do.

Except Gideon knew he wouldn't get answers over the phone. He was going to have to confront his father in person. Not wanting to waste time, he pulled his phone out and dialed his father's office. When his assistant answered, Gideon said, "Kim? I need to know my father's schedule."

"For when?" Kim asked.

"Today and tomorrow. I'm going to fly in for a meeting with him."

"Um... hold on." There was a click and then silence. Gideon stared at the cobbled sidewalk as he continued to walk along the Main Street shops. "Gideon?" Kim asked. "Are you still there?"

"Yep."

"I'm sorry, but it looks like your father has already left for the holidays. He won't be available until after the new year. Do you want me to put something on the books?"

"He already left?" Gideon asked, astounded. That would mean his father was going to be out of the office for over three weeks. That was unheard of.

"Yes. He came in this morning, passed out the Christmas bonuses, and then gathered some paperwork and left. He said he's taking his wife somewhere warm and doesn't want to be bothered unless there is a literal fire burning the office down."

"Son of a... Do you know where they are going? He told me Costa Rica, but do you know what resort they are staying at?" The chances were more than good that Kim had made their reservations.

"Nope. He wouldn't even tell me that much. He said he'd handle the details himself."

Gideon froze. "You're kidding."

She sighed. "I'm not. Your best bet is to call him yourself if it's important. If I do it, I'm likely to get fired. He wasn't joking around."

Kim had worked for Gideon's father long enough to know not to call his bluff. He couldn't blame her for not wanting to bother him when he'd told her under no uncertain terms that he didn't want to hear about anything unless it was a true emergency. "I'll call him. Thanks, Kim, and happy holidays."

"Thanks," she said, sounding relieved. "And happy holidays to you, too."

After he ended the call with Kim, he called the one person he knew in Los Angeles who'd be willing to dig up information, just as long as Gideon was willing to write a few checks.

"Gid!" the jovial man yelled into Gideon's ear when he answered the call. "Long time, no talk. What do you need?"

"For you to be discreet," Gideon said.

"When am I not discreet?" Baker asked, sounding offended.

Gideon scoffed at the PI who'd become the go-to investigator for anything having to do with Hollywood. "That time you walked into Heather Vee's dressing room and told her you were hired to track down her past lovers."

Baker let out a bark of laughter. "That's because my client was a jackass and had no business looking into Heather's past. And the only reason I didn't quit that job was because the dude threatened me. You know that."

"Right. I forgot about that." Gideon blew out a breath. "Listen, I need you to find out the major players on a film that's being produced by Witching Hour Productions."

"Is there a reason why you can't just call them up and ask?"

It was a fair question. For just about any other project, he likely could make one phone call and have all the details he ever needed. "I tried that. I'm being stonewalled."

"That's unusual. Who'd you piss off?" Baker asked with a chuckle.

"No one that I know of, but here's the kicker..." He clutched the phone tighter before adding, "My father appears to be self-financing it."

"Throm Alexander is financing a film produced by Witching Hour?" he asked, confused. "Why would he do that?"

"Yes, Throm is putting up the money. As for why he'd do such a thing, that's why I'm hiring you."

"What the hell is it? A porn flick?" he asked with a laugh.

Gideon couldn't help the chuckle that escaped his lips. Baker was one of those guys with no filter. He said whatever was on his mind, no matter how inappropriate. "Nope. It's a romantic comedy. Or at least it was until the screenwriter got ahold of it. Now it looks more like a tragedy."

The investigator's tone lost all traces of humor as confusion creeped in. "That does not sound like a Throm Alexander film."

"No, it doesn't." Gideon went on to explain Miranda, her book, and how it was about his and Miranda's relationship

ESSENCE OF THE WITCH

while they were in college so that the investigator had the full picture.

"I take it your father didn't approve of Miranda?" Baker asked.

"It's not that he didn't approve of her. He just didn't approve of the life I was leading when I was with her. Long story short, he wanted me to work for Ace Media, and I wanted to open an art gallery. Obviously, Throm got what he wanted."

"Maybe not everything or he wouldn't have his fingers in Miranda's movie."

"I can't imagine what that might be," Gideon said honestly. He knew his father had tried to block Miranda's book from being published, but he'd always assumed that was just a bargaining chip to get Gideon to toe the line.

"That's what you're hiring me for, to figure out what questions to ask and then fill in the blanks. Do you have a timeframe on this?"

"As soon as possible. Before the holidays would be best. They're supposed to start filming right after the new year."

"Okay, but there's going to be a rush fee," Baker said.

Of course there was. "Fine. Bill me directly. Don't send it to the office."

"You got it, boss."

The call ended, and Gideon had an intense desire to toss the phone into the nearby river. He'd spent far too much time on the damned thing in the past twenty-four hours, and he had little to show for it. But instead, he tucked it into his pocket and headed for Incantation Café. He arrived just before closing and ended up being Hanna's last customer of the day.

Twenty minutes later, with two lattes and two Danishes,

Gideon got into his SUV and headed for a small cabin on the edge of the woods.

It wasn't long before Gideon was knocking on Miranda's door.

The door swung open and there she was, dressed in jeans and a sweatshirt with her hair piled up on the top of her head and a pencil tucked behind one ear. "Gideon!" she said and glanced down at herself, grimacing. "You could've given me some warning so I could get cleaned up."

He took a moment to scan the length of her body. She was all comfort and curves. "There was no need for that. You look just as gorgeous as ever."

Miranda rolled her eyes, but then she focused on the coffee tray in his hand. "Is one of those for me?"

"Yep. Lattes and Danishes. I wouldn't show up empty-handed."

Her grimace turned to a smile, and she held the door open wider for him. "Then by all means, get in here. You have no idea how much I was craving a really good latte."

Gideon followed her inside and set the coffee and Danishes on the bar in her kitchen. "I found out who the screenwriter is."

She spun around to face him. "You did? How?"

"Through the grapevine." He handed her a business card with Troy Bix's name on the back. "I didn't call him, as per your request. This is just for you or your lawyer if you need to get in touch with him."

Miranda's hand trembled as she took the card.

Gideon took a closer look at her. "Are you all right?"

She shook her head. "I thought I was, but then I heard the name of the person who butchered our story and… I dunno. I'm back to hating everyone, especially my former agent."

She spun around in the kitchen and opened one of her cabinets. After moving a few things around, she pulled out a mortar and pestle. She started searching through another cabinet, inspecting her supply of herbs and roots.

"What are you looking for?" Gideon asked.

"My stash of Spanish moss."

His eyebrows shot up. Spanish moss was used mostly in hexes and curses. "Why?"

Miranda sucked in a sharp breath then closed the cabinet without extracting any of her jars. When she turned around, her face was bright red, and she stared at her stocking feet as she said, "I was planning on hexing Olivia."

"Cast a bad luck spell?" He let out a small chuckle. "I thought you were a pacifist earth witch. When's the last time you cast a hex on someone, Miranda?"

Her eyes snapped up to meet his. "I think I was thirteen. And it rebounded so badly that I ended up with a bad case of acne that didn't fully clear up for about a year."

"It's probably best not to mess with the hexes." He winked at her. "Karma will get Olivia in the end, and nothing will bounce back on you."

Miranda sighed. "Yeah. I guess you're right." She opened her fridge and pulled out a pitcher of green juice. "I'll just have to stick to the chill potion I made earlier." After she poured herself a glass, she glanced at Gideon. "Want some?"

He thought it over. Considering his angst over his father since the day before, it might not be a bad idea. But the slightly frothy green liquid smelled like a combination of dirt and fresh cut grass, neither of which were at all appetizing. He shook his head. "I'll stick with the latte."

"Suit yourself." She returned the chill potion to the refrigerator, picked up her glass, and handed Gideon his latte. After touching the edge of her glass to his coffee cup, she said, "Bottoms up."

Gideon took a sip of his coffee while he watched her down her potion. He couldn't help grinning at her. She was exactly who she'd always been, uninhibited, full of fire, and cute as hell. He was glad he'd stopped by. Seeing her, being around her, just made him more relaxed. The tension had drained out of him. He'd forgotten that she'd always had that effect on him.

"Want the Danish I brought you?" he asked, pulling one out of the bag.

"Not right now," she said with a lopsided smile.

He wasn't the only one who'd shed the tension. Her shoulders had eased, and the stress lines around her eyes had vanished.

Miranda grabbed his hand and tugged him over to the couch. "Sit," she ordered.

Gideon didn't need to be told twice. He leaned back against the velvet cushions and finished off the excellent Danish.

"Gideon?" Miranda said.

He turned to find her staring at his mouth. His breath caught as he watched her lean in and lick her lips. "Yeah?" he breathed.

"You, um…" She giggled and then her tongue darted out, licking the corner of his mouth. She made a show of tasting whatever was on her tongue and then touched the corner of her own mouth. "You had some cream cheese filling there."

"So, you thought you'd just take care of it for me with your tongue?"

Her eyes twinkled as she nodded. "It was delicious, too."

"You're delicious," he said, brushing back a lock of hair

that had fallen out of her bun. That connection that had always sparked between them was stronger than ever. One hand landed on her outer thigh while the other one cupped her cheek.

She stared into his eyes, vulnerability shining back at him. "I've missed you, Gideon."

"Same here," he said, even though he hadn't meant to. If they allowed themselves to come back together, they'd be walking into a minefield of problems. But Gideon wasn't sure he cared. His entire body buzzed with the need to be with her, to hold her close, to make her *his* again.

"Gideeeeon," she said, her voice high-pitched. "You were always the one who got away. You know that, right? And why don't you have a Facebook page or Instagram page? You made it impossible for me to stalk you online."

Completely amused, he pulled away and studied her flushed face and glassy eyes.

She tried to lean back into him, her lips aiming for his.

It took all of his willpower to put a hand out and stop her. "This probably isn't a good idea, Mandy," he said gently.

"A lot of really good things start off with a bad idea," she mumbled and reached for the buttons on his shirt.

"Whoa, sweetheart," he said and gently wrapped his fingers around hers, stopping her. "I don't think we should do this right now."

"Why?" Her eyes narrowed in challenge. "What are you afraid of?"

Everything? And nothing. He wanted her more than he wanted his next breath. But it was clear she was drunk off the chill potion she'd made, and no way was he letting things get heated while she wasn't fully sober. "I think it's better if we pick this back up after the potion wears off."

She climbed to her feet, glaring at him. "We won't be picking this back up, Gideon. You had your chance. Now and then." She closed her eyes and pointed to the front door. "I think you should just leave."

The last thing he wanted to do was walk out and leave her. But he didn't really have a choice if she was throwing him out. He got to his feet and moved toward her.

She took a step back, shaking her head. "Nope. We're done here."

"All right." He shoved his hands in his pockets so he wouldn't be tempted to try to touch her again. "I'll call you later to make sure you're okay."

"You really don't need to do that." She spun, presumably heading for her front door, but her footing was off and she tripped, landing awkwardly in the nearby chair. "Oomph!"

Gideon was by her side instantly, gently tugging her back up to her feet.

She mumbled something incoherent as she slumped against him.

"Miranda? Are you all right?"

"Fine." She gazed up at him, her eyes closing. Her words were slurred as she added, "I think I drank too much potion."

"Maybe. Do you need help getting to bed?" He knew she'd told him to leave, but she was in no condition to take care of herself at that moment.

"Just help to the bedroom," she said, eyeing the stairs.

"You got it." In one swift motion, Gideon swept her up into his arms and carried her up the stairs to her bedroom. There were twinkle lights around the windows and covering the four-poster bed. It really was like sleeping in a fairy cottage. He placed her gently on her bed with her head resting on the pillow. "Do you need anything?"

"Just you," she said so softly he barely heard her.

"You've already got me," he whispered.

She curled onto her side and patted the bed beside her. "Stay."

He was about to tell her he shouldn't when she reached for his hand and laced her fingers between his. Her eyes closed again, and he had the feeling that if he left, she'd sleep just like that, on top of the covers in her jeans and sweatshirt. "Miranda?"

She didn't move.

"Hey." He wiggled her hand a little, causing her to pull her hand back and tuck it close to her body. Okay, time for plan B. He could see a T-shirt poking out from underneath her sweatshirt, so he reached down and lifted her into a sitting position.

Her eyes fluttered open but didn't focus on him. Instead she said something about being hot. That wasn't a surprise. The upstairs was warmer than the downstairs, and she was drunk on a potion.

"I've got you, Mandy. Can you raise your arms over your head for me?"

To his surprise she did as he asked, and he was able to quickly divest her of the sweatshirt. "Do you want to stay in those jeans?"

She glanced down at herself and shook her head. Then before he could do anything, she wiggled out of them and tossed them on the floor.

"Um..." He tried to look anywhere except at her bare thighs and the red silk and lace that peeked out from beneath the hem of her T-shirt.

"Now I'm cold," she said, curling into a ball.

"We need to get you under the covers." He flipped one

side down and then helped her roll over until he could tuck her in. "There. Is that better?"

She nodded but then shook her head as she patted the bed next to her. "Stay."

Gideon knew he could leave and she'd probably be just fine. But considering how fast the potion had hit her and how out of character she was acting, he had a powerful urge to watch over her. "Okay."

Her eyes fluttered closed again, and a small smile claimed her lips.

Gideon disappeared into her bathroom for a few minutes. When he returned to her side, he was wearing only a T-shirt and boxers. Not wanting to cross any boundaries, he laid down on top of the covers and used a quilt at the end of the bed to cover himself.

Miranda reached out and placed her palm on his chest. Before long, her breathing evened out and it became obvious she'd fallen into a deep sleep.

Gideon, however, was acutely aware that the one woman he'd ever loved was curled up beside him. He covered her hand with his and didn't care in the least that sleep evaded him. He wouldn't miss this moment for the world.

CHAPTER 13

*M*iranda woke with a start. Her head was pounding and her stomach queasy. What had she done the night before? She rolled out of bed and stumbled into her bathroom. After taking a quick shower, she wrapped herself in a thick robe, stuffed her feet into her fuzzy slippers, and gingerly made her way downstairs. But before she even got halfway down, she heard the clang of dishes and froze.

Someone or something was in her house. Her heart started to pound against her breastbone and her head spun. Should she run back upstairs or bolt for the front door? Her feet were glued to the stairs, and fight-or-flight function had completely failed her.

"Miranda?" Gideon's voice floated from the kitchen.

She blew out a relieved breath and then felt her entire body heat with embarrassment.

Holy hell, *what had she done last night?*

"Um, yeah," she croaked out and forced herself to move.

When she got to the bottom of the steps, she tightened the belt on her robe.

"Hey there," Gideon said, smiling at her. "How are you feeling?"

She cleared her throat and tried to forget that her hair was wet and she likely looked like a drowned rat. "To tell you the truth, I'm a little under the weather."

His smile vanished. "I thought that might be the case. That chill potion hit you pretty hard last night."

Flashbacks of downing the frothy green drink ran through her mind. And had she thrown herself at him? Her stomach rolled and she pressed one hand to her belly. "What exactly happened?"

Gideon passed her a mug of what looked to be some sort of herbal tea. "Not much. After you drank the potion, you got pretty loopy. I was going to take off, but then it became obvious you could use a little help, so I put you to bed."

"And where did you sleep?" She sniffed the lemon herb tea and took a small sip. Immediately her stomach settled. "Oh, thank the gods for this."

"You're welcome." He flipped a piece of french toast onto a plate and added a couple pieces of bacon. Once he had the second plate done, he grabbed them both and put them on the bar counter. "I slept next to you on the bed."

She closed her eyes, mortified. "I assume I invited you to stay over?"

He chuckled. "You did. But don't worry. All we did was sleep, and you didn't do anything embarrassing."

Relief rushed straight to her toes. It wasn't that she was against doing anything physical with Gideon, she just didn't want to do it when she was too intoxicated to remember it. Not that Gideon would take advantage of her in that way.

He'd done exactly what she'd expect from him; he'd made sure she was okay and kept an eye on her. "Thank you."

He reached across the bar and pushed her wet bangs out of her eyes. "You have nothing to thank me for. All I did was help you get upstairs and then hog the left side of your bed."

"The left side, huh? Well, at least you still remember which side is mine and which is yours."

His lips curved into a slow smile. "Trust me when I say that is something I'm never going to forget."

He was flirting with her and so help her, she loved it. How could she make sure their banter never ended? "How do you feel about blue balls?"

His eyebrows shot up as his eyes widened. "I'm sorry. Did you ask me how I feel about blue balls?"

She cackled. "Yes."

He glanced down as if checking out his own package. "Can't say I'm a huge fan."

Snickering, she took a seat at the bar and picked up a fork. "I thought you'd say that. That's why I think we should go with red and gold."

He poured himself a cup of coffee and then gestured to the pot, asking if she wanted one.

"Yes, please."

He gave her his mug and then filled another for himself. Once he was seated, he said, "Okay, explain the balls. What are we talking about?"

"We need to decide what colors to decorate with for the Christmas ball. It's either silver and blue or red and gold. I kinda like the richness of red and gold, myself."

Gideon nodded. "Definitely. How about we turn the ball into an art fair of sorts? You know, decorate it with original holiday art. It can either just be on display or for sale."

"For charity!" Miranda slipped off the stool and hurried over to a drawer where she retrieved a pad and pen. After scribbling some notes, she sat back down in front of her breakfast. "That was an excellent idea. We can source artists at the art market this weekend."

"Sounds like a plan."

Miranda turned to him, her nerves almost getting the better of her, but she had to ask. "Will you paint something?"

He put his fork down and turned to look her in the eye.

She was certain he was going to balk. After all, he hadn't been a professional artist for many years now.

But to her surprise, his eyes lit up and he grinned as he said, "Sure. I'd love to."

"Really?"

"Really. I even have a piece I've already been working on." He winked and took a sip of his coffee.

Miranda's heart soared. He really was an exceptional artist, and it had killed her when he'd given it up to be a suit for his dad's company. But it was only because she knew how he lit up inside when he was working on something special. She'd missed that part of him almost as much as she missed the relationship that they'd had. "I can't wait to see it."

His cheeks flushed, but his smile only widened.

"Thank you for breakfast," she said. "The french toast is amazing."

"You're welcome, Mandy."

Her heart melted at his use of the name he used to call her back in college. "And thank you for taking care of me last night. I know I made a fool of myself, but you—"

"You did not make a fool of yourself," he insisted. "The potion was just too strong. Don't give it another thought. It's not like I suffered. I'd sleep next to you every day of the week if that was an option."

Her breath caught. They'd been harmlessly flirting, but that statement had taken things to an entirely other level. She could go one of two ways; either she could laugh it off, or she could make it a challenge. Because it was Gideon, there really was no choice. "All you have to do is ask."

His eyes turned molten, and she was certain she saw a single flame spark to life in each eye. "Don't tempt me, Mandy."

That was it. Game over. Miranda got to her feet, took one of his hands in hers, and tugged him off his stool. Then she gave him a slow seductive smile and led him upstairs to the bed they'd shared the night before. But this time she wasn't going to forget a thing.

"Miranda," he breathed once she turned to him. "Are you sure about this?"

In answer, she untied the belt of her robe and it gapped open, revealing her naked skin.

Gideon let out a small gasp of need and then moved in, his large hands landing on her curvy hips. "You have no idea how much I've missed you."

The words were like a healing balm to her soul. Tears stung her eyes as his lips met hers, but she blinked them back as her body came alive under his touch. In the next moment her robe was gone, and she stood bare before him.

"Mandy," he said with a groan. "You're even more gorgeous than ever."

There was a time when she would've felt completely exposed standing naked before him while he was fully clothed. But not now. She only felt the awe reflected back at her through his gaze, and it filled her with pure power. Gideon was one hundred percent hers, and she knew it.

"Strip," she said, taking a step back to watch him.

He didn't hesitate. Their eyes met as he slowly divested himself of his button-down shirt and then his jeans. Pure desire mixed with intense emotions crackled between them. There was no denying that this moment was so much more than just physical. The words love, connection, and soul mate ran through her mind, but she didn't feel the need to voice them. They both knew what they meant to each other. It was just time to stop denying it.

Miranda let her gaze scan his fit body before she linked her fingers through his and guided him to her bed where they finally, after far too long, became one again.

CHAPTER 14

$\mathcal{G}$ ideon lay on his side with Mandy's back pressed against his front as he caressed her bare arm. They'd come together like two starved people who hadn't been able to get enough of each other. Their lovemaking had started slow and sweet and had quickly turned hurried and desperate and incredible. He pressed a kiss to her shoulder and had to swallow the promises on the tip of his tongue.

The truth was, he couldn't imagine walking away from her again, but he still didn't know how that would work. It would mean walking away from his life in Los Angeles, but he didn't know if he could do that. His entire life for the last decade and a half had been all about Ace Media. At first, he'd taken the job to appease his father. But it turned out he was good at his job, and while it didn't allow him to tap into his artistic side, he found it satisfying.

"Gideon?" she said.

He pressed his lips to her neck. "Yeah?"

"How come you aren't taken?"

"What?" he said with a chuckle.

Her hand covered his and she gently stroked his fingers. "Why aren't you married with two kids and a dog? Or why isn't there a hot aspiring actress blowing up your phone? You're a catch."

"I could ask you the same thing," he said, dodging her question. This definitely wasn't something he wanted to talk about, although he desperately wanted to know what was going on with her and Cameron Copeland.

"Kids? Really? You know I never was baby crazy," she said. "I do want a dog though. Now that I'm here in Keating Hollow, it seems like it's time for a puppy. Something small and cute like a maltese or a maltipoo."

"Yeah, you're definitely a dog person."

Miranda snuggled against him and pressed a kiss to his palm. "That was a pretty good swerve, but don't think I didn't notice how you sidestepped my question." She rolled over and pressed a palm to his cheek. "It's just not possible that a man like you was alone all these years."

Staring into her gorgeous kind eyes, Gideon said, "No. I wasn't alone. I've had three semi-serious relationships since we broke up, but none of them worked out."

"Semi-serious. What does that mean?" she asked. "Did you live together?"

He shook his head. "No. All three of the relationships crashed and burned about the time each of them was ready to take the next step from dating to cohabitating."

Miranda frowned as she studied him. "You didn't even want to try with any of them?"

How could he tell her that the only woman he'd ever wanted to live with was her? Now wasn't the time to confess that none of them had measured up to her. He didn't know what this was between them, and even if it was the start of a relationship, it was way too soon to be putting that kind of pressure on either of them. He settled for the simple truth. "I just wasn't in love with any of them."

"I see." Her gaze dropped to his lips, and pure magic sparked between them again.

"Miranda," he said so softly he wasn't sure she heard him.

But then she raised her gaze to his and said, "Yes?"

"What about you? Has there been anyone special in your life since… well, since college?" He didn't really want to know, but he hadn't been able to stop himself from asking.

"Yes." She pulled away from him and rolled onto her back as she stared up at her exposed-beam ceiling. "We were engaged."

Son of a… *dammit*. That hurt a hell of a lot more than he anticipated. But she had said *were*, hadn't she? As in past tense. "Who called it off?"

She chuckled. "You would ask that first."

Gideon propped himself up with an elbow, holding his head in his hand as he gazed down at her. "Well?"

"I did. Are you happy?"

Yes. "No. While it would've been hard to see you with another man, I did want you to find someone to love." That was the truth at least. He wasn't so selfish that he wanted her to spend her life alone.

"I had people to love, Gideon." She averted her eyes and her expression turned heartbreakingly sad when she added, "But they both left me."

It was like an arrow to the heart. *Both.* She'd said both. He knew without having to ask that she was talking about him and Cory. He wasn't romanticizing what he'd had with her. There was no doubt that they'd loved each other. Their breakup had been the hardest thing he'd ever gone through, and the real reason he'd never let himself fall for anyone else was because he'd never gotten over her. He squeezed her hand. "I am so sorry about Cory."

"I know. I'm sorry, too." She looked up at him with tears in her eyes. "Don't think I didn't know you two stayed friends."

A lump formed in his throat, and he swallowed it down. "I was there, you know. At the funeral."

She just nodded.

Of course she'd known. "I wanted to say hello to you, but I just... couldn't. It had already been too emotional of a day."

Her tears spilled down her temples. "I know, Gideon. I know."

He gently wiped her tears away and then kissed both of her temples. "And I'm sorry I left. I'm so effing sorry."

She let out a strangled laugh. "I know that, too."

He didn't know what else to say, so he laid down flat on the bed and pulled her into his arms where she belonged. Everything with her just felt right, even when they were talking about their pasts and ex-lovers. *This,* he thought. This is what was missing in his life.

She hugged him tightly and whispered, "I called it off because it just wasn't right. It wasn't... I know what it means to be head-over-heels in love, and at some point, I realized I was settling." Miranda lifted her head and gave him a shaky smile. "Can you imagine a romance author settling?"

"Absolutely not, Mandy. You deserve your own epic love story."

She sighed into his neck. "Yeah. I thought so, too."

An ache formed in his chest. *He* was her epic love story, dammit. She shouldn't have had to contemplate settling with anyone. Was it too late to change things now? After what they just shared, he didn't think so. But after breaking her heart once before, he just didn't know if he was too late to rewrite their history.

MIRANDA PULLED AWAY and sat up. "On that note, I need to get showered. I have somewhere to be in an hour."

"Somewhere to be?" he asked.

After cloaking herself in her robe again, she glanced over at him. "I told Cameron Copeland I'd meet him for lunch today."

"Oh. I see." He sat up and reached for his clothes as she disappeared into her bathroom. She had another date with Cameron Copeland. Damn, he was a fool. Did he really think he could waltz back into her life, fall into bed with her, and then everything would be forgiven? It was more likely that she'd just had a moment of weakness.

Gideon yanked his clothes back on and trudged downstairs where he went to work on cleaning her kitchen. Neither of them had eaten much of the breakfast he'd made, so he put the french toast and bacon into a plastic container and poured out the cold coffee that was still in the coffee pot. By the time he had the dishes loaded in the dishwasher and the counters cleaned off, Miranda was headed back downstairs in a red and black corset dress. Damn, she looked good.

Doing his best to hide his jealousy, he grabbed his keys from the counter and moved to stand in front of her at the bottom of the stairs. "I'll get out of your hair now."

She glanced up and smiled at him. "Thanks for... well, everything. Taking care of me last night and this morning and…" She waved a hand up the stairs and blushed. "That was nice, too."

He couldn't help it. She was too freakin' adorable. And if she was going to go off and spend time with Cameron Copeland, he was going to make damned sure she was thinking about him the whole time. "It was more than nice, gorgeous. It was incredible." He wrapped one arm around her waist, pulled her in, and covered her mouth with his, giving her a deep, searing kiss that seemed to go on forever. By the time he let her go, they were both panting. "See you tonight," he said. "Seven o'clock at Mystyk Pizza."

She'd covered her mouth with her hand, and her eyes were wide with surprise. But still, she nodded and said, "Seven."

"Good." He gave her one last soft kiss on her lips and then left before she could say another word.

CHAPTER 15

*M*iranda sat in her car, trying to get control of herself. What the actual hell had happened back there in her cabin? She couldn't believe that not only had she fallen into bed with Gideon, she'd also just been kissed so senseless that she'd agreed to a date that she knew she shouldn't accept. What was she doing? He was going to shatter her heart again, and it would be all her fault. She was the one who invited him to her bedroom, stripped, and then ordered him to join her.

"Ugh." She held her head in her hands and vowed to keep her distance. They'd work on the Christmas ball together, but other than that, she had to stay away. She needed to find a way to keep herself busy. Otherwise, she knew she'd end up right back in bed with him. All of her self-control had flown out the window. She just couldn't help it. That thing, whatever it was that was between them, hadn't diminished. If anything, it felt even stronger to her because now she knew just how rare it was.

"Girlfriend time. That's what I need." Not that it was

going to help her later that night. Why had she agreed to dinner with him? Right. The Christmas ball. What had she gotten herself into?

She fumbled for her phone and called Shannon.

"Hey, Miranda. What's up?" Shannon asked. "Any news from Tim?"

"Not yet. He's working on getting my payments in order and establishing a connection with the studio so that I can give my input. But that will take a bit of time, I'm guessing." She jammed her key into the ignition. "I was actually calling to see what you're up to tomorrow night. Any chance of a girls' night? I need a distraction."

"Actually, I'm getting together with Hope to go over some wedding planning. You can join us if you want."

Miranda swallowed a groan. Did she really want to hang out with two women who were planning their weddings? It wasn't that she didn't like weddings. She actually usually enjoyed them, but with Gideon's reappearance she feared looking at wedding magazines would be pure torture. Still, it was better than the alternative. "Yeah, sure. Where? Your house?"

"Hope's actually. If you bring the wine, I'll bring the pasta."

"Don't you think we should check with her first?" Miranda asked, not wanting to intrude.

"Nah. She was already talking about asking Abby and Yvette to come, too. It's mostly going to be wine and discussing menus."

"All right. Thanks for the invite."

"Anytime, Miranda," Shannon said. "You're one of us now."

Miranda's heart swelled with affection. She hadn't had

very many close friends over the years. Not the kind that lived in town and got together regularly, anyway. Most of her friends were writers, and they lived all over the country. It felt good to have a girl group that she really liked to spend time with. "Thanks. That means a lot."

"Don't mention it. See you tomorrow."

Miranda ended the call, and feeling a little more in control, she put the car in drive and made her way into town, grateful it hadn't taken days to get her car fixed. The problem had been some sort of sensor that hadn't taken any time at all to change. She was just happy to have her car back.

Cameron Copeland was sitting at a table near the front window of Incantation Café. Miranda strode over and set her laptop down before shedding her coat and hanging it up on a nearby coatrack. "Hey. Do you want me to get you something? I need a coffee before we get started."

"Sure." He rattled off his order and immediately turned his attention back to his computer screen as his fingers flew over the keys.

Miranda smiled to herself and took off for the counter without another word. She recognized the signs of a writer engrossed in an idea.

"Hey, you," Hanna said from behind the counter. She glanced at Cameron and pumped her eyebrows. "Hot date?"

"More like a grueling work session," Miranda countered with a smile. "We're collaborating together on a project."

Hanna gave a slow nod, looking impressed. "Nice." She eyed Cameron. "He's kind of a big deal, right? Shannon said he's had a few hit movies."

Miranda let out a bark of laughter. "Yeah. He is. But who

knows if this project will go anywhere? I'm just happy to get the experience."

"Good luck. Whatever happens, it's exciting." Hanna handed her two drinks and two coffee cake squares.

"Thanks." Once Miranda was seated, she set the latte and coffee cake in front of Cameron and then waited patiently for him to finish typing. His fingers were flying rapidly over the keys, and his look of concentration was one she knew well. It was what she called 'the zone.' And she'd be damned if she interrupted him.

While she waited, she opened her laptop and answered some business emails. She was just getting ready to open a Word doc to jot down some notes for her next novel when Cameron finally came up for air.

"Yes. That's it." He grinned at her. "I just figured out the season arc, a twist, and a cliff-hanger ending."

"Wow." Miranda sat back, impressed. "So that's what all that intense writer energy was all about."

He chuckled and glanced down at the paper cup in front of him. "Is that mine?"

"Yep. But I'm not sure you need it." She gave him a lopsided smile. "Considering how you were pounding on the keyboard I'm guessing more caffeine probably isn't recommended."

He scoffed. "I'm a writer. There is no such thing as too much caffeine."

Miranda couldn't fault his logic there. On long writing days, she was known to go through a pot all by herself, too. "Fair enough. Are you going to show me your genius?"

Cameron pushed his laptop toward her. Miranda took a few minutes to read over his notes and by the time she was done, her jaw was left hanging open and her pulse had quickened. His treatment was amazing. Better than anything she'd seen on television lately.

"Cameron," she breathed. "This is... I don't even know what to say about it. It wrecked me. All the emotion. All the feels. Damn, you're good."

He gave her a slow smile, the kind that said he knew exactly just how great his work was. But then it vanished as he turned serious. "I have to confess that the idea came from something you said when we were at dinner the other night."

"Oh, yeah?" A trickle of pride lit her up inside. "What did I say?"

"You said the arc should run deep within the family. That the curse should be tied to all four brothers and that each one of them would have to overcome something in order to break it. So I ran with that. Each season can feature the struggle of one brother trying to defeat his portion of the curse. For season one, I decided that the oldest brother falls for the daughter of the curse-maker and the second-oldest brother is the best friend of the same girl. Then the eldest brother will have to sacrifice his soul for the soul of one of the other two, and that's how we end up here with the cliff-hanger. Will he save the soul of his younger brother or the girl he loves? It's an impossible choice. And in season two, he can deal with the emotional trauma while brother two walks his own journey."

Miranda loved the story. It was emotional, full of impossible choices and ambiguous morality, and ultimately was about love and the curse of the human condition. "This is full of everything I love to watch on television. I just hope there's space for it in the market right now."

"I guess we'll find out." Cameron moved his chair so that

they were sitting side by side, their heads bent together while they filled in the details of his treatment.

Four hours later, mentally exhausted and overly caffeinated, Miranda sat back and stretched her arms over her head. "I think we've got it."

Cameron nodded, his eyes lit with excitement.

Miranda chuckled as she watched him fire off an excited email to his agent. "I can't believe you're so energized. I feel like we've run a marathon."

"I always get like this when I know something has come together just right."

"And how do those projects usually turn out?" she asked.

"Do you mean, do they usually get picked up?" he asked, eyeing her.

"Yes." She laughed. "That's exactly what I'm asking."

"Always. And trust me when I say that I'm one hundred percent confident this project will not be the exception." He winked at her and fired off another email to a producer he'd told her he'd worked with in the past.

"Careful, Cameron. You're going to get my hopes up," she said, trying and failing to remain calm. It was impossible when he was so obviously giddy and confident. She couldn't help the anticipation and euphoria of possibility. Working with Cameron, who was well respected and connected, had her believing that anything was possible.

His phone buzzed with an incoming message and Cameron's eyes started to gleam as he said, "You *should* have high hopes, Miranda. There's a ninety-five percent chance that your dreams are about to come true." He turned the phone around so that she could see the message. It read, *Just saw your email. Call my assistant for a meeting next week.*

ESSENCE OF THE WITCH

"Who is that from?" she asked, barely able to get the words out.

"My producer friend. He works for SpellBound Entertainment. He told me last month they were looking for a paranormal drama. If he likes it, we're in."

Miranda just stared at him for a long moment, her mouth hanging open. Was this really happening? Was this real life? These kinds of things didn't happen to her. Sure, she'd been published with varying degrees of success, but she'd spent most of her career flying under the radar and fighting for every book contract. And when that went south, she took control of her writing career and started publishing her books herself. It was a decent living, and she certainly was grateful for her modest success.

But having a movie in production that was based on one of her books and collaborating with Cameron Copeland on a series that might be picked up by SpellBound? Both were a complete fantasy come true. She let out a little squeal, threw her arms around Cameron, and gave him a big smack on the lips. "Cameron Copeland, I think I just fell in love with you."

CHAPTER 16

I think I just fell in love with you. The statement, along with the image of Miranda and Cameron locked in an embrace, ran through Gideon's mind. He'd just stepped into the Incantation Café when he saw Miranda wrap her arms around the man.

His world shrank to just the two of them, and everything inside of him turned to stone. Hadn't she just been in his arms a few hours ago? And now she was hanging all over Cameron. He cleared his throat and strode over.

"Miranda?" he said, coolly.

"Gideon." She quickly pulled away from Cameron and her face flushed pink. "You're not going to believe—"

"Can I talk to you for a minute?" he asked, cutting her off.

"Um, okay." She glanced at Cameron and then got to her feet.

"Hey, man," Cameron said. "You okay?"

Gideon barely looked at him as he ground out, "Perfect."

"Yeah, you sound like it." Cameron chuckled to himself.

Gideon felt the urge to growl at the other man but managed to contain himself as he walked outside.

Miranda grabbed her wool coat from the coat rack and followed him. Before he could say anything, she asked, "What the hell is wrong with you?"

"Me? Nothing other than finding you with—" He stopped abruptly. What was he doing? Yes, he'd spent the morning with Miranda in her bed, but they weren't a couple. They hadn't even broached the subject of exclusivity or anything close to a relationship. He had no right to be angry with her. "I'm sorry. You don't owe me any explanations. I should go." He turned, intending to leave her be, but Miranda caught his hand and stopped him.

"Wait," she said.

He let out a slow breath and turned to face her, but he didn't say anything. He didn't have any words. The pain of seeing her with Cameron was still a fresh wound, but it was pain he didn't have a right to feel.

"Cameron and I are working on a script for a television show. That's why we were meeting today," she said, staring him in the eye.

Gideon held her gaze, his body still tense with jealousy. He rolled his shoulders, trying to relax, to let it go, but he was still too keyed up. "You are?"

"Yes." She gave him a small smile. "He has a producer who is interested. They're meeting next week."

"Who is it?" he asked automatically. In his line of work, it was second nature.

She laughed. "Why? Do you think you might want to bid for the project?"

He didn't even know what the television show was, but just knowing that Cameron and Miranda had created it, his interest was more than piqued. "Maybe. I'd love to hear about it, anyway."

She chuckled. "We'll have to loop Cameron in on this discussion, but I bet that can be arranged."

"Script, huh?" he asked as he once again replayed the scene of her throwing her arms around Cameron and proclaiming her love for him. In hindsight, it looked a heck of a lot more like a spontaneous display of affection than a declaration of love. Holy hell, he was an idiot.

"Yeah. Script." She threw her head back and laughed.

This time it was his turn to flush red. But then he narrowed his eyes at her. "Hey, if all you were doing was working, then why did you get embarrassed when I walked in the café?"

"Seriously?" She rolled her eyes. "Because the first thing I thought of when I saw you was being bare-assed naked and ordering you to strip. I suspect I'm going to be flushing about that memory for a long time."

"Oh." His face heated even more, and he was sure he'd turned a lovely shade of tomato-red. "I think that particular memory is going to become a favorite of mine."

Her eyes twinkled in the late afternoon sunlight as she moved in and pressed one hand to his cheek. "You're a piece of work. You know that, right?"

He nodded. She was right, after all. He'd gone all caveman on her, and now he felt like an idiot. "Is it too condescending to say I'm proud of you? Your books are incredible, and it's amazing that *Witching for You* is being turned into a movie, even if the studio is effing it up. And now you're working with Cameron Copeland. Do you have any idea how huge that is?"

"I know," she said softly, leaning in to rest her head on his shoulder. "It's pretty overwhelming actually, but I'm determined to take a step back and enjoy it. And as for you saying you're proud of me, no, it's not condescending at all. Thank you."

He ran a hand over her thick, dark curls. "I think it's safe to say that I'm not okay with either of us dating other people right now."

She pulled back, her eyes wide as her mouth worked, but no words came out.

"I know I don't have a right to be making demands," he said, unable to believe that he'd just told her he wanted to be exclusive. They'd just reconnected. He didn't even have any idea how long he was going to be in town. Yet there he was, making a claim. He couldn't help it. They belonged together. There was a reason why none of his other relationships had worked out, and that reason was standing right in front of him.

"It's okay. You're right," she finally said. "If we're going to do this, it should be just us. No dating anyone else. For either of us."

The emphasis she put on the words *either of us* had him grinning. She hated the idea of him dating other people. It was written all over her face. "So, we're doing this then? Dating only each other until..." He lifted his hands and shrugged his shoulders. "I guess we'll cross that bridge when we come to it."

"Right." She smiled, but it didn't reach her eyes.

Dammit. He knew that look was because he'd hurt her before when he'd walked away, and she was probably thinking it would happen again. But the thought of leaving Miranda Moon made bile rise into the back of his throat. He'd done it before, but now he had the benefit of knowing what it would be like to lose her. He wasn't eager to experience that pain again.

Gideon tightened his arms around her and pulled her in close. "Let's not think about the future for now," he said into her ear. "How about we just enjoy each other and Christmas in Keating Hollow."

"I can do that," she said, twisting her head to glance up at him. "Christmas really is magical in this town. And it's going to be even better once we get this ball planned."

"It'll be the best Christmas ball this town has ever seen," he said. The truth was he couldn't care less about the ball. He only wanted to spend time with the woman he'd never stopped loving. If that meant planning a charity ball, then bring on the mulled wine and candy canes. Whatever it took, he was there for it.

"You bet your tight as—erm—buns." Her eyes were twinkling again, even as a gust of wind picked up and made her shiver.

"You're cold." He tugged her back toward the café. "Let's get you inside so you can get warm before we head to dinner."

She didn't hesitate. Once they were back inside, Miranda shed her coat again, revealing her gorgeous curves. Gideon couldn't take his eyes off her, and he started to wonder if they needed dinner at all. Maybe they could just get takeout and go back to her house.

"Looks like you two worked out your differences," Cameron said, standing and shoving his laptop into a case.

"Huh?" Gideon asked like an idiot.

The other man rolled his eyes. "Everyone saw the way you two were looking at each other out there. I'm glad

Miranda's happy, but you know you acted like a class-A douche when you walked in here, right?"

Gideon nodded because it was the truth.

"She doesn't deserve that. Treat her right, okay?"

Who was this guy? He was acting like her big brother or some sort of father figure. Still, the man spoke the truth, and Gideon found himself nodding. "There's no question."

"I hope not." He glanced at Miranda and said, "I'll call you when I know more. Have a good night."

"You, too. And thanks again, Cameron. This has been amazing for me."

"Right back at ya." Cameron waved at her, winked at Gideon, and then disappeared out into the cold without anything more than a long-sleeved cotton T-shirt to protect him from the chill.

"He's hardcore," a woman said from behind them.

Gideon turned to the woman wearing a lowcut red sweater, tight black jeans, and knee-high, spiked-heel boots. Her bright-red hair was kind of wild, and she wore a dazzling smile.

"Hi, I'm Wanda," she said, holding her hand out. "You must be Gideon."

Gideon raised his eyebrows. "Sounds like I have a reputation already."

Wanda laughed, the infectious sound filling the room. "Keating Hollow is a small town. It's not every day an attractive single man shows up out of the blue for no apparent reason." She winked at Miranda. "Unless of course your reason for visiting is the lovely lady standing next to you."

In fact, Gideon hadn't known Miranda was in town, but she had become the reason he hadn't already moved on. "I was only planning on staying a few days, but this place seems to have a hold on me."

"Place or person?" She grinned, clearly not expecting an answer, and focused her attention on Miranda. "Hey, you. I've been meaning to tell you I have a decoration crew all lined up for the ball. They're just waiting for instructions."

Miranda reached out and hugged the other woman. "You're a gift from the gods. Thank you. We're going over things tonight. I'll let you know our game plan sometime tomorrow. Does that work?"

"It's perfect." Wanda gestured to a golf cart parked in a spot in front of the café. "I'm off for my weekly race with Abby. Did you hear that witch put a hex on Rosie? My turbo boosters just stopped working, and then the headlights started rotating all over the place, turning them into some strange version of disco lights. It's impossible to see anything down at the river with that nonsense. She'd better be ready, because I'm bringing the fire this time."

Miranda laughed. "Just don't blow anything up, okay?"

"Killjoy." Wanda waved to Gideon as she started to retreat. "Have fun tonight kids. Don't do anything I wouldn't do."

Gideon was still staring after her when he said, "Somehow, I get the feeling that list isn't very long."

"I think you're right." Miranda slipped her hand into his. "Ready?"

He pressed a kiss to her cheek, nodded, and led her back out into the cold.

CHAPTER 17

*M*iranda was overwhelmed. Utterly and completely overwhelmed. Her day had been packed full of emotion. She'd started out worried about the movie, fell into bed with Gideon, felt the start of another dream-come-true while working with Cameron, and now she was in an exclusive relationship with Gideon.

It was a lot.

And she didn't have any headspace to process any of it. Not that she had the opportunity at the moment. She and Gideon were knee-deep in Christmas ball planning. They'd shared a margherita pizza and a bottle of red wine while working on the menu and bar options. The food would be served on floating trays at various spots at the ball, while the champagne and other drinks would just magically appear in the glasses when the guests voiced their choices.

"Why are there hot wings on this list?" Gideon asked her with a fair bit of side-eye. "No one is going to want to get sauce all over their face while wearing black tie."

She snickered. "You're not wrong about that. They were a

request from Levi. He said something about Silas hating all the stuffy parties he has to go to and how he wished that just once an event would surprise him with wings and beer. So that's for him."

"That's actually pretty sweet," Gideon said.

"It is, isn't it?" Miranda couldn't help but think of Cory when talking about Levi and Silas. He'd had a sweet teenage romance just like theirs. She'd always thought the two would find their way back together, but then the worst had happened. For years she'd wanted to rewrite his story, center him in a romance, and give him the happily-ever-after that he deserved, but she still wasn't ready. One day, she'd get there.

Miranda flipped open the notebook just as the waitress brought them another basket of sourdough bread that she'd asked for. "Thank you," Miranda said, smiling at the waitress as she picked up the breadknife and reached for the basket.

"Son of a—ouch!" Gideon howled and slammed back against the booth, holding his hand to his chest.

Miranda's limbs froze with shock as she watched blood soak his hand. "What the heck happened?"

His gaze fixated on the knife still in her hand. "You stabbed me with that thing."

She glanced at it, finding a smear of blood on the sharp edge. What? How had she stabbed him? She'd just been holding the knife, hadn't she? Maybe she'd moved it while reaching for the bread? The how didn't matter, though. Gideon was bleeding, and every cell in her body tingled to help him.

Miranda had been a healer at one point in her life, but she'd quickly learned she didn't have the energy to keep up with healing patients on a daily basis. It was too draining.

She dropped the knife, reached across the table, and grabbed both of his hands in hers. Magic bubbled to her fingertips and swirled inside of her like a storm. It had always been that way. She didn't have the ability to only use what was needed. Her magic ripped through her, coating his hands and making them glow for a moment before the magic vanished.

"How is it? Did the bleeding stop?" she asked him.

Gideon gingerly opened his good hand and looked down at the cut finger. "Yes, but this wound is going to need attention."

Miranda nodded, reached into her purse, and pulled out a wad of bills. "Yep. I'm not skilled enough to do more than staunch the bleeding. Time to get to the healer."

"Oh my gosh, sir," the waitress gasped as she appeared at their table. "Are you all right? Can I get you anything?"

"A clean towel?" he asked.

"Of course." She darted away and was back in the blink of an eye with a white towel. "Here. Just take it. The meal's on us."

Miranda gestured to the money on the table. "There's no need to do that. This was my fault. Thanks for your help." Then she placed her hand on Gideon's arm and led him out of the restaurant. Once they were in her car, she said, "I'm so sorry about that. I don't even know what happened."

"Me either." He rested his head against the seat and closed his eyes. "First fire and now knives. Remind me to keep the poisonous herbs and roots away from you." He sent her a tiny smile.

Miranda knew he was joking, but for the love of the goddess, what was happening to her? Had she been on a date in recent memory when something hadn't gone horribly wrong? The only time something hadn't gone wrong lately was when she'd been with Cameron. Except those had been work sessions. The one time she was supposed to have been on a date with him, he'd stood her up. Then she'd lit his assistant's hair on fire. Her other recent disasters included being set up with her cousin, her car breaking down, and now she'd almost cut Gideon's finger off. He was right to be worried.

Miranda grimaced. "I'm a walking disaster."

Gideon reached out with his uninjured hand and squeezed her thigh. "But you're my walking disaster."

"Oh, man. That was really sweet." She lightly squeezed his fingers and then brought them up to her lips and kissed them lightly. "Thanks for making me feel better."

He moved his hand and cupped the back of her head as she drove the short distance to the healer's office.

Miranda led the way into the healing clinic and strode up to the reception desk. To her surprise, Gerry Whipple, one of the healers, was behind the desk.

Gerry looked up and smiled at Miranda. But the smile quickly vanished, and her lips curved down as her expression turned to one of concern. "Honey, where did that dark aura come from?"

"What?" Miranda asked, glancing around as if she could see what the healer was talking about.

"You've got some sort of bad juju going on. Feels kind of like a sour love spell. Let me get you back into one of the offices so we can take a look."

"Wait. That's not why I'm here." She gestured to Gideon, though a bad love spell would explain so much. She just had no idea where she would've gotten it. Miranda didn't mess with love spells. If she was going to fall for someone, it wasn't going to have anything to do with a spell. "He has a finger that probably needs some stitches."

Gerry stretched her neck to see around Miranda. "Oh, I see. Well, good thing you brought him in then; otherwise you might not have known, and things could've gotten really unpleasant for you and the people around you."

"I think we're already there," Miranda said dryly. "I'm the one who accidentally stabbed him."

"Oh, sweetie," she said, shaking her head. "Did this happen on your date?"

"Yes." Miranda sighed. At least now she knew for sure why all her dates had been going south. And yet, she and Gideon had still managed to get together. That knowledge soothed her and even made her a little hopeful. If she had a botched love spell affecting her life and it hadn't stopped them from starting up again, then anything could happen, right?

"That makes sense. Okay, let's get you both fixed up." A younger woman appeared from the back and took Gerry's place at the desk as the healer led them both back into the patient area. "Here you go, Miranda. You take a seat, and I'll be right back after I get your young man situated with Martin."

Gideon let out a small chuckle, no doubt amused by her 'young man' comment.

"I'm sorry," Miranda said again.

"I know," Gideon said, his expression still amused. "It's going to be fine."

"Yes, it is," Gerry confirmed, holding the door open for him. "Martin will have that finger fixed up in no time."

Miranda sat back on the patient chair and closed her eyes as she waited for Gerry to return. Who in the hell had cursed her love life and when? As far as she knew, she didn't have any enemies. She felt sick thinking about it, but if Gerry was able to clear her energy, she would be grateful. An involuntary shudder ran through her as she considered how long her aura must've been tainted. Her "date" with her cousin had been weeks ago. If it had been allowed to fester, she hated to think what might've happened the next time Gideon took her out. Her entire body started to shake from the horror of feeling violated.

There was a knock on the door, followed quickly by Gerry entering the exam room. The older woman gave Miranda a wide smile. "I'm back." She grabbed a pair of latex gloves and tugged them on. "Now, let's see what we can do about this spell-gone-wrong."

Miranda sucked in a breath and let it out slowly. "You said my aura had a dark tinge. What else do you see?"

"Not much. Looks like your aura is usually a pale rainbow, but right now the colors are muddy due to this broken spell. But don't worry, I can fix that." She opened the door to a cooler and retrieved what looked to be a potion and set it to the side. Then she sat on a rolling stool and glided over to Miranda. "Let me get a better feel for what we're looking at."

"Okay." Miranda sat in the reclining chair, just waiting.

"Relax, Miranda," Gerry soothed as she took Miranda's hand in hers. "I thought you had training in healing?"

"I did, yeah." Her entire body was still shaking with nervous energy, and it was starting to piss her off. She didn't want to break down in the healer's office.

"Then why the anxiety?" Gerry asked conversationally. Magic started to tingle over Miranda's skin, making her warm from the comforting sensation. "Did you have a bad experience with a healer once?"

Miranda shook her head. "I guess I'm just freaked out that I've been cursed and didn't know it. I was a healer but gave it up because healing drains me."

Gerry nodded. "That tracks with what I'm sensing. I think you've been hit with a love spell that went sideways, which means it's not likely someone was trying to curse you on purpose. If I had to guess, they were trying one out but didn't have the skill to make it work and it got away from them and never got neutralized. It's not strong enough for you to notice a difference in your energy. You might have been a little more tired lately, or emotional, or even just more sensitive. Does any of that seem plausible?"

The shaking stopped and Miranda sagged in relief. "Yes. I've had a lot of big stuff happening in my life recently. I just thought it was because of that. If you can help me get back to functioning at my normal levels, I might just adopt you as my new best friend."

Gerry chuckled. "I'd never turn down an offer for a good friend." She got up and retrieved a few jars of herbs from one of the cabinets. After carefully measuring and mixing them with the base potion, she shook it hard and then handed it to Miranda. "This should do the trick. It might make you a little nauseated, but it's more likely you might be light-headed or sleepy. I'd drink it a few hours before bed. And then to be safe, I'd do a very thorough smudging of your living area and workspaces to make sure none of the spell is lingering anywhere."

"I work from—" She started to say she worked from home, but then realized she'd spent most of the last few months at A Spoonful of Magic working on her last manuscript. Miranda made a note to talk to Shannon about cleansing the store, too. She gave Gerry a whisper of a smile. "Turns out I spend most of my time working somewhere else. But I'll make sure we get that space, too."

Gerry nodded once. "Good. This should work just fine, but you should get your aura read in the next few days just to make sure."

Miranda hopped off the table, the potion still clutched in her hand, and said, "Thanks, Gerry. I really appreciate your help. How long do you think Gideon will be?"

She chuckled. "You'd already done half the work with that healer magic of yours. I bet he's already waiting for you out front."

Even though all Gerry had done was zap her with a little bit of magic to read her energy and the broken spell, Miranda already felt like a ten-pound weight had been lifted off her shoulders. The knowledge that a spell had been messing with her was actually a relief. It meant that, hopefully, now her dating life wouldn't be one disaster after another.

A smile claimed her lips when she saw Gideon waiting for her by the reception desk. His finger was bandaged with just a couple of butterfly strips. She glanced at it. "That's all you needed?"

"Two stitches. The dissolvable kind." He shrugged one shoulder. "It turns out your magic helped seal the wound, so it's not that big of a deal."

Miranda stepped into his arms and hugged him. "I'm so glad. I'm mortified."

He stroked her back with his uninjured hand. "There's no reason to be embarrassed. Now, if you'd sliced the tip off and left it in the breadbasket, then maybe—"

She jerked back, grimacing up at him. "Eww. That's not right."

He laughed. "Come on, Mandy. Let's pay up and get out of here. Then you can tell me all about your aura issues."

She groaned. "You're not going to believe this."

"Believe what?" he asked as he led her outside to her car.

"All this crap that keeps happening?" She waved at his hand. "The car breaking down, setting that guy's hair on fire, it was all because I'm cursed with a broken love spell."

Gideon blinked. Then he started to laugh.

"Hey!" She took a step back, fighting the urge to whack him in the shoulder. She'd done enough damage for one day.

"I'm sorry, Miranda," he said, those blue eyes of his shining at her. He took a step closer and pulled her into him, pressing his body to hers as he whispered in her ear, "I'm only laughing because I feel like I should thank whoever did this. It meant you were right here waiting for me when I finally found you again."

A shiver overtook her entire body, and her limbs started to tingle with her reawakened magic.

"You're practically vibrating," he said, running a hand down her arm.

She smiled up at him. "It's your fault. Your touch does things to me."

His lips turned into a sexy little half smile. "Well, not yet, but it will." He pressed a soft kiss to her lips but quickly let her go and said, "Hold that thought." Then he opened the car door for her. "Let's go home."

Home. Her home. The one she'd gladly share with him for as long as he wanted. She had to fight to hold back the pesky emotions that were bubbling at the surface of her heart. "Yes. Home."

CHAPTER 18

"Can I do anything else for you?" Gideon asked Miranda, trying not to panic. She was sitting on her bed, holding her head with one hand and her stomach with the other.

"Water?" she croaked out as her skin turned green.

And a bucket, he thought. If she made it through the next few hours without vomiting, it was going to be a miracle.

Once they'd gotten back to her house, they'd wasted no time diving into an intense make-out session. He'd been ready to drag her to bed, but she'd stopped him to explain the treatment for the bad spell she was still carrying around with her. So he'd reluctantly let her go and volunteered to smudge the downstairs floor of her house while she drank the potion.

It had been a while since he'd smudged anything, but he knew the drill. He had to burn a spelled sage stick, ask any unwanted energy to leave, and then smudge the entire house. By the time he was done, the house felt warmer and more welcoming.

Except when he'd gotten upstairs to check on Miranda, she looked like death had touched her. All he'd wanted to do was crawl into bed with her and hold her, but the nausea had prevented that.

He hurried from the bedroom, got her a bottle of water, and found a bucket just in case.

"Oh, gods," Miranda said when she saw the bucket, and she closed her eyes.

"Sorry. I just thought it was better to have it handy in case you needed it," he said, handing her the water.

"It's fine," she said. "You're right. But the thought of…" She closed her eyes again and concentrated on breathing.

Gideon pulled out his phone and called the healer. Once he explained the situation, he asked, "Is ginger tea all right? I want to give her something for the nausea."

"That should be fine. It's better to keep the potion in. If she vomits it back up, she'll just need to drink another one."

Gideon decided to keep that tidbit to himself. She sure didn't need to be thinking about that. "Okay. I'll make her some tea then."

"Gideon?" the healer said.

"Yeah?"

"If it gets worse, call me," she said, sounding concerned.

"What do you mean, worse? Like if she's vomiting?"

"Yes," she said. "Vomiting, migraine, any signs of distress. It's not unusual to feel nauseated or have a slight headache, but if the symptoms are severe, it's a problem."

"Okay. I'll keep an eye on her." Gideon ended the call and made his way into the kitchen where he made her a ginger tea. Then he went back upstairs. He found Miranda curled on her side with her eyes closed and her head propped up on two pillows.

"Hey, you," he said, sitting on the bed next to her. "Any better?"

"Not really," she mumbled.

"I have tea. Healer Gerry said it should help." He stroked her arm gently, just for reassurance for them both that she was going to be okay.

"You called Gerry?" she asked, pushing herself up into a sitting position.

"Yeah. I wanted to make you a tea to help the nausea and needed to make sure it was okay. Is that all right?"

She gave him the tiniest of smiles, making his heart feel full. "Yes. Thank you for doing that and for the tea." Miranda took the mug with both hands and sipped. She grimaced. "It has a bite."

"It's the ginger."

"I know," she said, shaking her head. "I'm an earth witch. I know my roots."

"Sorry." He held his hands up in the air and laughed. "Of course you do." He moved to sit on the other side of the bed and waited as she sipped the tea. "Better?"

"I think so." She set the mug on the nightstand and burrowed down into her covers.

Gideon leaned over and kissed her temple. "I need to stay over. Is that all right with you?"

She opened one eye and peered at him. "Need?"

Chuckling, he brushed a lock of hair out of her eyes. "Yes. Need. Gerry said I should keep an eye on you, and I can't do that from my room at the inn. Plus, I want to stay and take care of you."

"Oh." Her lips seemed to be curved into a permanent ghost of a smile. When she continued, her voice was barely a whisper. "So, it's Gerry's fault?"

"If we need someone to blame, sure. But I'm not denying that I don't want to leave this bed."

"Oh, you're sleeping with me too?" Her tone was teasing now.

Gideon got up off the bed, shucked out of his jeans and Henley shirt, crawled back into the bed, laid down flat on his back, and pulled the thick down comforter over them. Lifting it slightly, he patted his chest. "Come here. Let me hold you."

Miranda didn't hesitate. She tucked herself beside him and rested her head on his shoulder. And then she did the thing she'd always done way back in college. She hugged him tightly and let out a contented sigh.

Damn, if that didn't hit him in all of his feels.

He tangled his fingers in her hair, kissed her gently on the lips, and then closed his eyes to revel in the moment. She was everything he wanted. He knew that now. His life back in Los Angeles meant nothing without her. Whatever it took, he was going to find a way to make their relationship work, even if he had to sell everything and move to Keating Hollow.

He smiled at the thought, held onto Miranda tighter, and when he heard her steady breathing indicating she was already deeply under, he let the night take him.

CHAPTER 19

*M*iranda woke with a start. Something wasn't right. She didn't know what it was, but there was an internal alarm going off in her head that was flashing a warning sign. The bed was warm but her hands weren't, and there was some sort of clacking noise that disoriented her. Her eyes flew open and she blinked, trying to process what she saw right beside her.

"Gideon?" Miranda bolted upright, staring down at her pale bedpartner. His skin had turned a ghastly shade of white, and his teeth were chattering as if he were freezing. "Gideon," she tried again. When he didn't answer, she pressed her hand to his head and cursed as she fumbled for the phone on her nightstand.

She quickly searched her contacts for Healer Gerry.

Gerry answered on the first ring. "Gerry Whipple."

"Gerry, it's Miranda Moon."

"Good morning, Miranda. How's your energy today?" the healer asked.

"There's something wrong with Gideon. I just woke up

and he's shivering, burning up, and unresponsive. I don't even think I can get him downstairs and in the car to get him anywhere."

"I'm grabbing my keys. Text me your address. I'm on my way." The line went dead.

Miranda immediately did as the healer asked. Then she tossed the phone to the side and pressed both hands to his cheeks. "Gideon. Open your eyes, baby. Come on. Look at me."

He let out a moan and tried to curl in on himself.

Panic started to set in, but as she stared down at the man she'd never stopped loving, she pushed her emotions to the side and concentrated, forcing magic into her fingertips. She knew she didn't have enough healing power to cure whatever was ailing him. He was just too sick. But she might be able to ease a bit of his suffering.

Sucking in a deep, cleansing breath, Miranda focused on her fingertips, letting her magic pool into them. Then she imagined Gideon healthy, his skin slightly flushed and wearing an easy smile as he walked with her in the woods the other day. When she held his healthy image firmly in her mind, she said, "Let this magic give Gideon the strength he needs to heal and overcome this illness."

Her magic poured over him, cooling his feverish skin, and instantly his teeth stopped chattering. He let out another moan as his eyes fluttered open.

"Hey, you," she said, her voice shaky. "Good morning."

He blinked a few times, his mouth opening as if to speak, but no words came out. He cleared his throat and winced as one hand flew to his neck. "What happened?" he rasped, barely audible.

"Looks like you picked up a nasty flu or something." She

brushed his dark hair back and leaned down to press her lips to his forehead. He was still burning up, but at least he was responsive. It was something, and something was a hell of a lot more than she'd had five minutes ago.

"Flu?' He squinted at her, looking confused. "I don't think —" Gideon tried to sit up, but quickly abandoned the effort and said, "Whoa. Why is the world spinning?" Then he looked down at his bandaged hand, the one she hadn't even thought to check, and his eyes widened with dismay.

"Oh, crap," Miranda said when she spotted the angry red swelling. The cut was infected. There was no doubt about it. And then fear set in. If he was sick from an infection, he was in serious danger.

"I need to see the healer," Gideon said even as he closed his eyes and laid back down on his pillow.

"She's on her way." Miranda climbed out of the bed and disappeared into her bathroom, where she retrieved a cool wet cloth. She didn't want to give him any medication for his fever before Gerry arrived, but the cool cloth should help. "Here," she said, climbing back onto the bed and placing it on his forehead.

He didn't say anything. He didn't move either, and If it weren't for the steady rise and fall of his chest, she might've worried whether he was even still there with her. Tears stung her eyes at the thought of losing him, and this time she did nothing to curb her emotions. Her face was wet as she made her way downstairs in her thick robe and fuzzy slippers.

After putting the teakettle on the stove, Miranda sat at her bar with her head in her hands and let out all the tension, fear, and frustration of the last few days. The absolute terror she'd felt when she'd woken up that morning was still simmering beneath the surface, and right then, nothing else mattered to her. Not her books, the movie, the television show. All she wanted was for Gideon to be all right. She'd done this. That stupid curse that she'd picked up and never realized she had was to blame. What kind of an earth witch was she anyway? An oblivious one.

The teakettle started to whistle, and she got up to make a restorative tea, but before she could even make it to the stove, her front door banged open and Gerry hustled in carrying an old-fashioned leather doctor's bag.

"Where is he? Upstairs?" Gerry asked even as she veered for the staircase.

"Yes." Miranda flipped the burner off and hurried after the healer. "I used some magic to try to start the healing process. He stopped shivering and woke up, but he doesn't look any better. I don't know what else I could've done. I was going to make a restorative tea, but now that you're here... just tell me what you need."

"You did great, Miranda," she said, looking slightly relieved. "If he woke up and was coherent at all, then you are a rock star, especially considering your healing limitations."

Miranda let out a small sigh of relief, but even that reassurance didn't really make her feel better. She wasn't going to be able to do anything but worry about Gideon until she was sure he was out of the woods.

They found Gideon burrowed in the covers, and his color was just as bad as it had been when Miranda had woken up, and he was shivering again.

Gerry took a seat on the bed and tugged the comforter back, exposing his barely clad body. She pressed her hands to his cheeks just as Miranda had. But instead of trying to talk to him, she started to chant under her breath and magic spilled from her, coating Gideon's entire body with a golden sheen.

His eyes popped open, and his body stiffened as all of his muscles tensed.

"Is he allergic to any medications? Specifically, turmeric based medications?"

"I don't know. I don't think so," Miranda said. "But it's been a number of years since we spent significant time together. We need to ask him."

"Okay." Gerry went to work, hooking him up to an IV and injecting something into the line.

"Can I do anything?" Miranda asked, hating that she was just standing there watching Gideon suffer.

"Yeah." Gerry handed her a tube of some sort of salve. "Undo the bandage on his finger and put this on the wound."

Her stomach rolled, but not because she was afraid to work on his injured hand. That was nothing compared to what she'd seen and done while studying to be a healer. It was because she was responsible for his current state, and nothing she'd done so far had seemed to help him. But the task Gerry had given her was a basic one, and even Miranda could handle it without messing up.

While Miranda worked on his infected finger, Gerry stood and continued to chant and monitor the potion level in the IV bag. "Just a little more, Gideon," she said under her breath. Miranda had just gotten the salve on Gideon's finger when Gerry nodded at the IV bag as if satisfied and then raised her arms in the air.

"Goddess of healing, come to us, lay your heart and hand upon this man. Free his physical body of the toxins suffocating him and fill his lungs with a fresh start. Fix the mistakes and show mercy for us both."

Fix the mistakes? Miranda was completely taken aback. What mistakes?

Magic crackled around the room, flashing like tiny bolts of lightning that hung in the air. And when Gerry swept her arms down and pressed her hands to Gideon's chest, the tiny bolts shot through the air and right into Gideon. The glow around his body turned such a bright red that Miranda had to shield her eyes before the layer hardened like a shell and shattered into tiny pieces that faded away into the ether.

Gerry stared down at Gideon.

Miranda, who was still holding Gideon's hand, squeezed slightly and said, "Gideon?"

His eyelids popped open, and his gaze darted around the room. He was frowning, and his expression was full of confusion until his gaze finally landed on Miranda. The change in his body language was palpable. His face relaxed, and a tiny smile claimed his lips. "Hey there. How are you feeling this morning?"

"Better than you." She gestured to his hand, the one she was still holding. "Your cut became infected, and Gerry had to flex her considerable magic muscles to get you back online."

His gaze traveled to his finger that was swollen and covered with a salve. "The cut made me that sick?"

"No," Gerry said. "You had an allergic reaction to the salve Martin used on your cut that was supposed to stimulate healing. If Miranda hadn't been here and called me, there's a very good possibility you wouldn't have survived this. I'm going to write down the formula for the salve we used. You *must* tell any healer you see in the future about your allergy so this doesn't happen again."

Gideon seemed to be stunned into silence.

"He could've died?" Miranda whispered as her head spun with the news.

"Yes. That kind of reaction can be fatal." Gerry sat on the edge of the bed again and said, "I'm going to check your vitals to make sure you're stable."

"And if I am?" he asked, sitting up in the bed and pressing his good hand to his head.

"Headache?" Gerry asked, using a light to peer at his pupils.

"Yeah. It's kind of like a hangover."

"That's pretty normal after the amount of magic I used to counteract your allergic response. Don't worry about it unless the headache persists into tomorrow."

"Okay." Gideon sat propped in the bed while Gerry finished her examination.

"Looks good," Gerry finally said. "The only side effect seems to be the headache. That's pretty remarkable." She turned to Miranda. "He can have a simple pain potion every six hours if he needs it. Otherwise, just keep an eye on him. If he starts running a temperature, even a minor one, call me right away. Got it?"

Miranda nodded, "I will."

"Good." Turning back to Gideon she said, "I am so sorry. Reactions like that are really rare. Looks like the swelling in your finger is already going down, though. Hopefully by tomorrow you'll be back on your feet."

"I hope so, too," he said. "Thanks for bringing me back from the edge."

"You're welcome, but it's Miranda you should be thanking. Her quick thinking saved the day." Gerry unhooked the IV and collected her supplies. Once she had everything packed up, she squeezed Gideon's hand and told him to rest for at least a few days.

Miranda followed her downstairs and offered her some tea before she left.

Gerry shook her head. "I need to get back to the office. But thank you." She took a step to move toward the front door but then stopped and turned around to hug Miranda. "You're one hell of a witch," she whispered. "Thank the goddess for you."

When Miranda pulled back, she couldn't miss the tears in the healer's eyes and her own filled again. "Right back at you, Gerry. Thank you for saving the love of my life."

Gerry let out a small choked sound of emotion, wiped at her eyes and straightened her shoulders. "We all just do what we can, right?" She smiled. "By the way, your aura is a pretty pastel rainbow today. Looks like that curse is gone for good."

"That's good," Miranda said, nodding. "Now maybe I won't light anyone else's hair on fire just because they have the audacity to take me to dinner."

Gerry chuckled. After a moment, the two women shared a watery smile as Gerry collected her things and then quietly left the small cabin.

Miranda let out a slow breath, completely overwhelmed by the morning's events. She glanced up the stairs, but instead of heading back up to Gideon right away, she sank to the floor and sobbed.

CHAPTER 20

*G*ideon was completely drained. After the healer left, he slept fitfully on and off all day. In between naps, Miranda was there with tea or soup and plenty of affection. He could tell that the events of the morning had completely wrecked her, but the only thing he could do was hold her.

"That feels good," he said to her when he woke to find her sitting next to him and caressing his head.

"Has the headache gone away?" she asked. Her eyes were bloodshot, and her hair was a mess. She'd tied it up in a messy bun, but instead of looking casually chic like it usually did, today it resembled something more like a bird's nest. And dammit, if all of that didn't make him want her even more. She'd spent all day watching over him, worrying, and waiting on him hand and foot. It was time he returned the favor.

"It's mostly gone. I think a shower might help."

"I'll get the water started for you," she said.

He laughed and grabbed her hand, stopping her.

"Miranda," he said with a smile. "I'm a grown-ass man. I think I can manage turning on the shower."

"Of course you are," she said, giving him a sheepish smile. "It's just… I can't seem to stop hovering, I guess."

"In that case, how about you join me?" he gave her a wicked look.

"Shower? Together?" Her creamy cheeks heated and flushed a lovely shade of pink. "I guess that means someone *is* feeling better."

He chuckled and swung his feet out of the bed. But as soon as he stood, he swayed a little.

"Whoa, big boy," she said, steadying him. "You sure you're up for this? I could give you an old-fashioned sponge bath."

He snorted. "As fun as that might sound, I'd rather us both get in the shower." He took her by the hand and led her into the adjoining bathroom.

"What about that finger? Can you get it wet yet?" she asked.

He lifted his hand, showing off the now closed wound. Gerry's intense magic hadn't just healed his feverish state.

"You don't really think we're going to… you know," she said, eyeing the shower stall.

"Going to what?" he teased as he reached into the shower to turn on the spray.

"Get lucky. I think it's a little too risky considering we're both in a little bit of a weakened state." She raised an eyebrow as if to challenge him.

"Speak for yourself."

Miranda rolled her eyes but then said, "Shh, don't tell anyone, but I think you might be feeling slightly better."

"I think you might be right." He leaned in and kissed her lightly on the lips before moving to her jawline and down her neck to her collarbone. When she let out a little moan of pleasure, he slipped his hands under her T-shirt and tugged it over her head, leaving her upper body bare and glorious. His own body stirred to life, and even though he knew she was right about him being too weak to do much of anything physical, he welcomed the sensation. His desire made him feel alive and present, which was a nice change since he'd felt like he'd been floating in a dream state all day.

Miranda wrapped her arms around him, holding him close, making him feel like he was the luckiest man in the world. He decided he'd be content to stand there in her arms forever, but when she gave a tiny shiver and he noticed the gooseflesh on her arms, he quickly stripped them both of the rest of their clothes and tugged her into the shower.

He was careful to turn Miranda so that the hot spray cascaded down her back.

She closed her eyes and let out a moan of pleasure, one that had his body waking up and saying hello all over the place. But he ignored his libido and went to work on gently washing Miranda with her honey-scented soap. Her skin was soft and warm to his touch. Comforting. He could have stood there in the shower forever, touching and caressing her, but eventually the hot water would run out.

"Turn around," he said, grabbing the shampoo bottle.

She leaned in and gave him a slow kiss before turning into the spray.

"Your body is incredible, Mandy," he whispered, working the shampoo into her thick hair. "Your curves are driving me insane."

"And here I thought you had a thing for my hair," she teased.

"I do." He brought his hands down to her shoulders and

kneaded the muscles, easing her tension. After tasting her
sweet neck, he said, "I might be obsessed with all of you."

She chuckled. "If this is how you handle your obsession,
I'm all for it."

Gideon took his time, massaging Miranda's scalp, then
rinsing, conditioning, and making sure every bit of her was
taken care of. They talked and teased, falling back into an old
rhythm they'd had years ago as she took her turn exploring
his naked body with the honey-scented soap. And when her
fingers went to work on his scalp, washing his hair, he
thought he'd died and gone to heaven. Her touch was
incredible.

When they were finally done and the water started to
run cold, Gideon turned off the water and helped her
dry off, stopping intermittently to steal her kisses and
graze his lips over her naked body. She was enjoying
doing the same to him... until her phone started to
buzz.

"I better get that," she said, slipping into her robe. "It
could be Gerry." She quickly snatched up the phone and
grimaced when she saw the name. "Dammit. I forgot."

"Forgot what?" Gideon asked

Miranda held her hand up, indicating for him to wait for
her answer, and into the phone, she said, "Hey, Shannon. Am
I late? What time were we meeting tonight?"

Gideon glanced around for his clothes. His jeans and
Henley shirt had been placed on a chair in the corner, and
his boxer briefs were still in the bathroom where they'd left
them. He considered putting them back on but rejected the
idea. He'd sweated right through them during his feverish
ordeal. He'd rather go commando than put them back on his
clean body. Instead he headed for his jeans, but a quick scan

of them revealed they were bloodstained. It was his turn to grimace.

"Oh, okay. Sure. Let me just check something," Miranda said and then pulled the phone away from her ear and spoke to Gideon. "I was supposed to go to Hope's tonight for girls' night, but…" She let her gaze travel over his still naked body. Heat flashed in her eyes and she licked her lips.

Normally, Gideon would've been right there with her, but after the shower, he was feeling a little worn out. The near-death experience had really taken its toll. "You should go. I'm not going to be good company anyway. I'll get dressed and head back to the inn."

"No," she said and pointed to the bed. "You're staying here so that I can keep an eye on you."

His lips twitched with amusement. "Really? Don't I get a say in this?"

"Nope. If you leave, I'll just follow you. Gerry said to watch you, so that's what I'm going to do."

He pursed his lips and nodded his head. "Okay, fine. I'll stay, but I do need to get some clean clothes and my toiletries from the inn. Is that acceptable?"

"I guess so." She said the words as if she were put out, but her smile gave her away as she pressed the phone to her ear. "Okay. It's all good. I'll meet you there in a half hour. Thanks for the call."

Gideon glanced at his bloodstained jeans again. If he was headed to the inn, he didn't have a choice, did he? He scooped them off the chair and quickly got dressed.

"You look like someone from *Night of the Living Dead*," she said, arching one eyebrow. "One wouldn't think that would be sexy, but it is."

He barked out a laugh and pulled her into him. "I missed

this."

"My sparkling personality and biting wit?" she asked, batting her eyelashes at him.

"Yes. And so much more." He gave her a slow, tender kiss, running his hands up her back. But before either of them could take it any further, he stepped back. "You need to get dressed, and I need to head to the inn."

She pushed her lower lip out in an exaggerated pout.

He chuckled, running his thumb over her bottom lip. "Later. Go have fun with your friends. I'll be here when you get back."

Her tongue darted out, tasting his thumb. And judging by the look in her eyes, he was certain she was going to blow off Shannon and fall back into bed with him. But she let out a frustrated groan and stepped back, putting some distance between them. "You're right. There are a couple of brides desperate for my opinion on their wedding festivities. We wouldn't want to disappoint them."

"Definitely not," he agreed, still thinking about dragging her to the bed.

She laughed, no doubt reading his mind. "Go." She gave him a tiny shove. "If you don't, I'm never going to stuff myself into my favorite jeans, dry this hair, or slap some makeup on. You need to go before I turn into the Cryptkeeper because I can't remember how to do a smoky eye."

Chuckling, he shook his head and said, "Now that really would be tragic."

"You have no idea." She flipped her wet hair over her shoulder and disappeared into the bathroom.

"See you later," he called and took off down the stairs. He had an overnight bag to pack.

CHAPTER 21

"*B*ut I don't want floating penises at my wedding," Shannon insisted as she wrinkled her nose. "Talk about tacky."

Shannon, Hope, Hanna, and Miranda were sitting on throw pillows around Hope's coffee table, trying to help Shannon decide what magical elements to incorporate into her and Brian's wedding on Valentine's Day. Shannon rolled her eyes when she explained it was the day Brian wanted, but no matter how put-upon she acted, that didn't stop the grin from creeping in, even when she was trying to hide it.

Hope sighed dramatically. "How many times do I have to tell you they are cupid-shaped candles, not penises. They just look like that because of the drip plate."

"It's a drip plate with lopsided balls," Shannon insisted.

Miranda sipped from the world's weakest margarita ever made and chuckled to herself.

"I hear you laughing over there, Miss Giggles. Don't think we didn't notice the dreamy look on your face when you got here." Shannon pointed a red-tipped finger at her. "You must spill. What *exactly* happened at Incantation Café between Gideon and Cameron? Hanna said Gideon looked like he wanted to scratch Cameron's eyes out and then punch him in the balls."

"That was... colorful," Miranda said diplomatically. "And it seems like a slight exaggeration of something Hanna would say."

Hanna cackled. "You're not wrong."

"Come on, spill it," Hope encouraged.

Miranda put her margarita down. "Weren't Abby and Yvette supposed to be here?"

"Nice dodge." Hope snickered. "Abby's too busy trying to get all her holiday orders out. Her new radiant skincare line is a huge hit. She's thinking she might even need to hire an assistant earth witch to help her keep up with demand."

"And Yvette?" Miranda eyed the pretty blonde, amazed at how things had worked out for her. It couldn't have been easy finding out you have four half-sisters and a half-brother all in the span of weeks. Going from having no family to being part of an iconic one in the town of Keating Hollow must have been overwhelming to say the least. But then, Miranda had come to learn that the Townsends were good people. Her friend Jacob had married well.

Hope's green eyes danced. "Brian volunteered to take Skye for the evening. They're making Christmas cookies, or rather Brian is making cookies and Skye is making a mess. But that left a quiet night alone for Jacob and Yvette. I bet they're dancing around the house naked already."

"I think that dance is called the horizontal mambo," Shannon said with a snicker.

The women raised their drinks in a salute to Jacob and

Yvette's date night. Miranda laughed and joined them. "Good for them."

Shannon picked up the magazine with the penis candles and then eyed Hope. "Would you order these for your wedding?"

Hope's cheeks flushed as she shrugged, giving a noncommittal response.

"It's not a matter of *would*," Hanna said as she threw her head back and laughed.

"What?" Shannon's brow furrowed as she turned to the café owner. "What does—omigod." Her eyes widened as she met Hope's eyes. "You already ordered these! But why? I thought your theme was casual elegance. These are…"

"Tacky," everyone but Hope said at the same time.

Hope's face flushed a deeper red as she said, "I was kinda tipsy when I placed the order. I don't know what I was thinking, but I thought they were little fairy candles. That would've been nice, right?"

"Sure. Fairies fluttering around the vineyard at night would've been very cool. Especially on New Year's Eve," Hanna reassured her. "But penis candles? Maybe they're more appropriate for Times Square."

"Or a strip club ceremony," Shannon teased. "Why are you trying to pawn them off on me?"

A bubble of laughter escaped Hope's lips as she nodded and then collapsed into a fit of giggles.

Miranda's body shook with laughter as she listened to the women talk about wedding plans and who was trying for babies and who wasn't. It was all very domestic, and while she enjoyed the time spent with them, she wondered if she really fit in with them. She'd never had a strong desire to have children. And the one man she'd wanted to spend the rest of her life with had never mentioned the word marriage. Not even when they were together in college. After watching his father work his way through four wives, it wasn't an institution he craved being a part of. Miranda could hardly blame him. So, she was single and likely to remain that way, which suited her fine. Mostly. Or it had until Gideon walked back into her life.

"Earth to Miranda!" Shannon called, waving a hand in front of her face. "You still with us, girl?"

Miranda blinked. "Huh?"

They all laughed.

"Are you dreaming about a certain Hollywood producer, or were you fantasizing about penis candles?"

"Neither," Miranda admitted.

Shannon raised one eyebrow in challenge.

Miranda laughed. "Okay, I definitely wasn't thinking about penis candles."

"So you *were* daydreaming about Mr. Charming," Hanna teased.

Miranda took another sip of her margarita. "I was thinking about him but not like that. I actually was just contemplating how you're all so domesticated now. Everyone's married or getting married and talking about starting families."

"Brian and I haven't talked about making babies," Shannon insisted.

"No, you just practice a lot," Hope said, chuckling into her glass.

"Don't we all?" Shannon grabbed a reindeer cookie off a tray and bit its head off.

"That's the truth." Hanna shrugged one of her shoulders. "I'd like to have kids someday, but I'm in no hurry. Abby,

Noel, Yvette, and Faith are the four who have babies on the brain. Yvette and Jacob have been trying, but so far, no luck. I think they're exploring the idea of adopting a sibling for Skye."

"I'm not in a hurry either. I have a teenager to raise," Hope said, referring to her half-brother who'd come to live with her earlier that year after being kicked out of his father's house and living on the streets for a short time. "And Chad and I just found each other again. Now isn't the time. But also, if we do decide on kids, I'm thinking about fostering and adoption as well."

Everyone turned quiet as they let Hope's words sink in. She'd spent most of her youth in foster care. It wasn't a surprise she'd feel strongly about building her family that way.

Hanna reached out and squeezed her friend's hand. "Levi's a great kid. You're doing a wonderful job."

Hope chuckled. "Levi *is* a great kid. But I can't take too much credit. He's just easygoing. And after everything he's been through, if anyone deserves to act out, it's him."

Miranda doubted Levi would give her problems. He was a tender soul, a spirit witch. They felt emotions deep in their bones, and there was no doubt he knew just how much Hope loved him. He was accepted, completely and fully, for the first time in his life by both Hope and Chad. It was the kind of love that healed a person.

"I don't think you have anything to worry about there, Hope," Shannon said. "But I might. Try managing your superstar teenage brother. Hollywood is hell on keeping egos in check." She winked, but there seemed to be genuine concern beneath her light teasing.

There were nods of agreement.

"We just need to keep him in Keating Hollow as much as possible," Hope said. "And not because he's dating my brother."

More chuckles.

"This town just isn't super impressed with celebrity," Shannon mused. "I do think it keeps him grounded."

The women continued to discuss their lives and loved ones and eventually moved back to wedding planning and taking bets on when the next Townsend baby was going to arrive. By the time the evening was over, Miranda still didn't have any answers to the questions she'd asked herself, but she knew deep in her soul that the women in that room were women she related to, and for the first time in her life, she felt connected to a place not only because of the beauty it possessed but also because of the people who'd embraced and accepted her for who she was.

Emotion swept through her and, not for the first time that day, she blinked back tears, only this time they were tears of happiness.

Miranda stood and raised her glass. "To friends, family, and penis candles!"

The other women followed her lead, and laughing, they repeated, "To friends, family, and penis candles!"

THE NEXT WEEK WAS INCREDIBLE. There was positive news from Cameron. The meeting he'd set up had gone well, and he told Miranda they should be seeing some sort of deal within days. Miranda was pleased but kept her expectations in check. She knew Hollywood was flakier than one of Julia Child's croissants. Besides, with the script problems for

Witching for You, the bloom was off the rose when it came to selling television and movie rights as far as she was concerned. In other words, she'd get excited when the contract was in her hot little hands and not a minute before.

She'd spent the week mostly working with Gideon on the Christmas ball. They'd decided to decorate the venue with rich red and gold and plenty of twinkle lights. Items were starting to be collected from the various town businesses for a silent auction, and Miranda was having a great time enlisting people to help enchant the venue. Some of the enchantments were perpetual snowfall that disappeared when it hit the ground, dancing snowmen, and animated ice sculptures.

But her absolute favorite feature was the customized gifts. Guests were to fill out a short questionnaire when they sat at their table for dinner, and a gift matching their personal taste would appear out of nowhere. It had been no small feat to pull it off, and she'd needed the help of an entire coven to put it together. The coven was actually based in Denver. Their leader, Bellini Bakarta, was a fellow novelist and an old friend of hers from years ago. Because Miranda had been Bellini's mentor once and her help had led directly to getting her start in publishing, Bellini had been eager to help.

Now there were stacks of enchanted gift boxes that had been sent from Denver and stored in the barn on the Pelshes' property, each spelled to conjure up unique gifts that were bound to dazzle the attendees of the ball. Miranda and the other committee members decided to hold the ball at the winery since they'd recently built a reception hall just for weddings and other special events.

It was Saturday morning, and Miranda and Gideon were

at the art market soliciting donations for the silent auction. Most of the artists were extremely generous, and Miranda had already secured forever-burning candles; handmade lotions that tanned, toned, and restored aging skin; and some witch-themed silver jewelry.

"There you are," Gideon said, falling in step beside her and wrapping his hand around hers. "We just scored an incredible piece of glass art that reads and reflects individual auras and a painting that echoes the scenery and weather of whatever location the owner wishes."

"Anywhere?" Miranda asked, smiling up at him. "That seems like a tall order."

He chuckled. "Okay, maybe not anywhere, but it will produce most scenery types. Desert, ocean, mountains, etc. You get the idea."

"Sounds great." She held up her bag. "I did pretty well over in the craft tent, too."

Miranda couldn't believe how effortlessly she and Gideon had come together again. After her curse had been obliterated and he'd recovered from his allergic reaction, they'd been inseparable. He'd even checked out of the inn and was staying at her cottage until… Well, she had no idea when he was leaving. He'd told her sometime in January when they'd talked about it last, but that had been before they'd dropped all their barriers and stopped fighting their connection.

"Check this out," Gideon said, tugging her over to another art glass booth. The artist had everything from platters and bowls to ornaments and suncatchers on display. "Look at this." He pointed to one of the suncatchers. "Stand in front of it and tell me what you see in the sunlight reflecting off the crystals."

Miranda smirked, expecting to see some sort of summer day scene or Christmas morning or just about anything that was designed to put a smile on someone's face. Instead, she saw herself and Gideon, their fingers linked as they sat in wooden Adirondack chairs overlooking the Keating Hollow valley. Only they weren't in their thirties. They were old, in their twilight years, both of them proud of their wrinkles and the proof of their long-lived life together.

Tears filled her eyes and emotion clogged her throat. Her free hand came up to cover her mouth as she sucked in a surprised breath.

"It's hard to see, isn't it?" a woman asked.

Miranda glanced over her shoulder at a slight woman in a long pencil skirt, form-fitting sweater, and a soft scarf around her neck to stave off the cold. Her short shag-style haircut was perfect for her oval face. Miranda didn't understand the question. The vision she saw in the rays of light couldn't have been clearer. "What's hard to see?"

"The thing that you want most in this life." The artist patted Miranda's arm. "It's not always that way, but when you're at a crossroads, sometimes the confirmation doesn't hold up to the goals we've been working so hard to achieve."

Miranda just stared at her, not quite sure what to make of her words. Was Miranda at a crossroads? She glanced at Gideon. If he decided to leave to go back to Hollywood, she definitely would be. But her vision was of her and Gideon together, in Keating Hollow, having lived a full life together. Did that mean she should follow him? Or that she should hold out for the life that she wanted?

The answer was obvious. She should follow him. And why wouldn't she? Her job meant she could work anywhere. Not to mention that if she continued collaborating with

Cameron Copeland, it would be easier for them to connect if she was in Los Angeles.

"Hey, Miranda," Gideon said, his deep voice soothing her nerves. "Are you all right?"

"Yes." She slipped her arm around his waist and snuggled in close. "I'm perfect, actually."

The artist beamed at them. "Lovely."

"Your work is gorgeous," Gideon said. "Do you sell it in any galleries?"

The artist's face lit up with excitement. "You know, before today I didn't. But the lovely owner of the Enchanted K Gallery came by and wants to put some in her store. We agreed to consignment, which isn't usually preferable, but she's local, so it's easy enough to keep an eye on things."

"You met Ashe?" Gideon asked, surprising Miranda. When had he met the gallery owner? And since when did that gallery start stocking anything other than the top 100 artists from *Niche* magazine?

"Yes. Just today actually. Sweet girl. We clicked right away." The artist wiped her hand on her skirt and then held it out to Gideon. "I'm Cleo."

"Gideon," he said, shaking her hand. "And this is Miranda."

Cleo turned to Miranda and flushed bright pink as she said, "I know who you are. Miranda Moon, right? *Witching for You* is my favorite book of all time. I just can't wait for the movie to come out. The ending… guh. I can't wait for my heart to be shattered and then put back together again."

Miranda forced a smile. She couldn't, even if she wanted to, explain that the movie would be different. She wasn't allowed to divulge details. So she thanked the woman, wished her luck on her art sales, and tugged Gideon away from her booth.

"Are you all right?" Gideon asked her.

She blew out a breath. "Yeah. That was... intense."

He let out a low chuckle. "Yes, it was."

Glancing up at him, she melted when she noticed he was staring down at her with a tender expression. "Did your vision line up with your life goals?"

He slowly shook his head. "Yours?"

"Nope. But I can't say I was disappointed."

"Me neither," he said and pulled her in closer. After pressing a kiss to the top of her head, he added, "Ready to go home? I was thinking a cup of cider by the fire might be nice right about now."

"Take out?" she asked.

"Burgers or pizza?"

She laughed. "Lasagna. I need to carb load before tonight's activities."

He laughed and then his eyes flashed with pure desire as his gaze scanned her body. It wasn't hard to catch her drift. They'd already planned to stay in since snow was predicted later that night. He pulled out his phone and placed the order with Woodlines. Then without another word, they held onto each other, quickly making their way to Gideon's SUV.

CHAPTER 22

The scene outside of Miranda's cabin the next morning looked like something that belonged on a greeting card. There was a fresh blanket of snow and a quiet peacefulness that Gideon felt all the way down to his bones. He stood at the back french doors watching as a magnificent buck stood off near one of the trees.

"He's glorious, isn't he?" Miranda said, handing him a mug of coffee.

Gideon draped his arm over her shoulders and pulled her against his half-naked body. Miranda kept the cabin warm enough that he was dressed only in sweatpants and a pair of socks. "Does he visit you often?"

"Only on significant days." Her fingers grazed his shoulder blade as she caressed his bare skin.

He eyed her and raised an eyebrow. "Really? Is he your spirit protector?"

She shrugged. "I don't know. But I noticed it a couple of months ago. Something profound or significant always happens when he comes to visit. His presence is a sign that change is coming, I think, because the events aren't *always* ones that I'm particularly thrilled about. Though sometimes they are. The last time I saw him was the day you showed up in town."

"I hope that was a good thing," he said with a laugh.

She pressed herself against him, kissed his jawline, and then murmured, "It took me a bit to decide, but I think I've landed on yes, it was a good thing."

"You think?" His hands gripped her waist, and the next thing he knew, he had her pressed up against the wall with her legs wrapped around him while he kissed her senseless. He was about to take her back to bed when his phone started buzzing with incoming texts from across the room where he'd left it on the counter.

"Ignore it," he said, kissing her neck and running one hand up her side.

"Okay," she breathed, letting her head rest against the wall as he tasted her lips once more.

The buzzing continued, and then the phone started to play the theme song from *Dexter*.

"Dark," Miranda said.

Gideon groaned and lowered her back down to the ground. "I have to get that."

"Leading a double life? Do you have a bad guy to take out?" She narrowed her eyes at him and pursed her lips. "You haven't turned into a vigilante serial killer yourself, have you?"

He laughed. "No. Sorry to disappoint. The ringtone is just assigned to a guy who gathers information for us so that we know what we're getting into when we start a new project."

Miranda frowned. "You mean a private investigator? You do that thorough a check on everyone?"

"Sometimes," he said with a shrug as he reached for the phone. "There's a lot of money at stake. No studio wants to eat millions of production dollars and then find out their star went on a racist rant... or worse."

"Fair enough." Miranda tugged on the sweater that she'd left on the couch and headed into her kitchen.

"Baker," Gideon said. "What do you have for me?"

"You're not going to like this," the investigator said.

Gideon had never had any illusions that he would. "I'm prepared for that. Lay it on me. What did you find out?"

"It's better if we don't do this over the phone. How soon can you get here?" Baker's tone was grave and carried none of the good-natured levity it usually had.

"You mean to Los Angeles?" Gideon asked, his shoulders tensing at the thought of leaving Miranda.

"Yes, unless you want to pay to fly me up there. But I'm guessing once you hear what I have to say, you're going to want to be here anyway."

Gideon's stomach started to ache with unease. "It's that sensitive?"

"Yes." Baker didn't need to spell out what he was implying. Whatever he'd found, it was sensitive enough he wasn't willing to share the details over an unsecured line. Sometimes the man crossed the line into pure paranoia, but he had good reason. More than once his phone had been bugged, and information he'd tracked down was leaked, causing major upheaval for a few stars. Information that was private and had no business being splashed into the public eye.

If Baker had learned something about his father that was unsavory, he was trying to protect Gideon from the news leaking. It was one of the reasons Gideon trusted him. "All right," Gideon relented. "I'll be on the next flight. I'll text you and let you know when to expect me."

"You know where to find me," Baker said and then ended the call.

"You're leaving to go back to Hollywood?" Miranda asked sharply. "What about the Christmas ball? You're supposed to be my date."

The warm, pliable woman who'd been in his arms only moments before had turned into a woman ready to hand him his ass. Her feistiness made him smile.

"Do not look at me like that, Gideon Alexander. This is not funny," she fumed. "I just got used to having you around, and I was supposed to get at least a few more weeks with you. This… leaving before Christmas thing is completely unacceptable. I can't believe—"

"Miranda," he said, stepping in close to her and wrapping his arms around her waist. "I do have to go, but I'll be back before the ball. I promise. One week from today, I'll be in my black tie and you'll be wearing something that makes you look like some sort of Christmas angel."

"You'll be gone a week?" she asked in a whisper. All of the fight had gone out of her, and now she just looked sad and disappointed.

"I hope not. My plan is to get down there and back again as soon as possible. If I even stay overnight, it will be too long."

She smirked. "Unless you charter a plane, I don't think there's much chance of flying down and back in one day. The Eureka airport only has two gates and one airline. Small is overstating things. Tiny is a better word."

"I'll just have to do the best I can." He kissed the top of her head. The last thing he wanted to do was head down to Los

Angeles, but he had to get to the bottom of his father's involvement with Miranda's movie. As he held her, he had a pang of guilt that he hadn't shared that news with her yet, but he really wanted to know the full story before he did that. He didn't want to upset her until they had answers, which was why he had to go figure out once and for all what his father's motives were for involving himself in a movie he had no business backing. "I need to go pack."

She sighed. "I was getting ready to make us pancakes. I guess that's out?"

He wanted to say no, it wasn't. But it was already past ten, and the roads were covered in snow. It was going to be a bear just getting to the airport. If it started to snow again, he might get stuck. "Raincheck?"

"Sure. I'll pack you something to eat on the way." She patted his chest and disengaged herself from his embrace.

"Wait," he said, grabbing her wrist.

Her expression was wary as she turned back to him. "Yeah?"

He tugged her in close, pressed a soft kiss to her lips, and said, "Thank you, Miranda."

"For what?"

"For taking care of me even though you hate the idea of me leaving. For sharing your home with me. For sharing your bed."

Her lips twitched into a smile.

"And for letting me love you after all these years. I'm not sure I deserved a second chance, but I'm damned grateful you gave me one."

"Oh, dammit, Gideon," she said as her eyes welled with tears. "You're a jackass."

He chuckled. "Why?"

She shook her head and then gave him an exasperated look. "Because here I was all set to be annoyed with you and then you go and say a thing like that. How am I supposed to stay upset after that declaration?"

Amused, he leaned down and kissed her softly. "I guess you'll just have to dig deep if you're determined to keep your hackles up. But if you're not, how about I FaceTime you tonight, and we can figure out what to do from there."

"I planned on taking a long bath in my soaker tub," she said.

His grin widened. "Perfect. You can take me with you."

"There will be bubbles and bath bombs. I don't think you're going to get to see as much as you think you are," she said and patted his chest. "But you can always hope for a glimpse between the bubbles, I guess."

"Sounds fun." He kissed her hard, leaving her breathless when he finally let her go. "Remember that when you're teasing me later."

"Um, okay." She pressed her fingertips to her lips and looked completely dazed. Her face was flushed, and he ached to finish what they'd started, but he needed to get to Los Angeles and see Baker. For her.

CHAPTER 23

"We did it!" Cameron raised his champagne glass to clink it with Miranda's. It was just after one in the afternoon, and they were at Woodlines celebrating their good fortune. "The contracts are vetted and all we need to do is sign."

"*You* did it," Miranda corrected, feeling somewhat like an imposter. Cameron had written the script. Sure, she'd given input, but she wasn't a screenwriter; she was a novelist. Surely he could've done all of this without her. "All I did was help with the storyline."

"Miranda," he said, rolling his eyes. "The main characters and the premise of the show are *your* creation. You were the one who helped me figure out the story arc. Without you, this show wouldn't be getting picked up by the number one streaming provider. Own it, sister. We did this together."

The imposter syndrome was strong, but his words cut through her resistance, and she grinned at him as she raised her glass to his. "We did it. We really created something magical."

"I think so." He winked at her, touched his glass to hers, and then downed half the glass.

Miranda grinned and took a long sip. Her fingers ached to reach for her phone. She'd just found out she and Cameron had sold their script, and the only person she wanted to tell was Gideon. Except, she'd already called and left him a couple of messages. Since he hadn't called or texted back, she could only assume that he was in a meeting with whomever he'd rushed down to Hollywood to see. Resentment bubbled up in her chest, and she had to work to push it back down.

The man had a job to do. She couldn't fault him for that. If he asked her to walk away from her career, she'd scoff and tell him to go to hell. If he needed to head home for work, then she'd be supportive. It's what a loving girlfriend would do. Was she his girlfriend? They hadn't explicitly talked about it, though they had discussed exclusivity and he'd thanked her for letting him love her. It wasn't that big of a leap to relationship status. She blew out a breath and wondered when she'd hear from him. He had called the night before, but she'd already been asleep. She had answered, but the call had been short because it was after midnight and they were both exhausted. It turned out he'd gotten the last flight out of Eureka, but it had been delayed due to weather.

"Miranda?" Cameron called. "You okay? Did you get lost thinking about what you're going to spend your newfound fortune on?"

She tilted her head and gave him her best shut-it look. "Fortune? While it's a good payout, I don't think either of us is getting rich off this deal... yet."

"There's potential," he said. "If it does well, we'll have a much bigger bargaining chip for next season."

She shrugged one shoulder. "I'm not counting any dollars until they're in my bank account."

Cameron raised his glass to her once more. "Smart lady. I knew there was a reason we work so well together."

"We both hear voices in our heads all the time?" she asked.

He let out a bark of laughter. "That's not quite what I meant, but I suppose there's some truth there too."

"Writers. We're a special breed." She chuckled and grabbed a piece of bread from the breadbasket just as their waitress brought their appetizers. She placed a goat cheese and honey salad in front of Miranda and a bowl of French onion soup in front of Cameron.

Just as Miranda picked up her fork, her phone buzzed. Anticipating that it was Gideon, she grabbed it and then paused when she saw the call was from Timothy, her lawyer. "Sorry," she said to Cameron. "I have to take this."

He waved her off, indicating it wasn't a big deal as she rose and headed outside. The cool air hit her as she stepped out onto the cobblestone sidewalk, and she tucked herself against the building to shield herself from the wind as she answered the call. "Hello?"

"Ms. Moon?" a woman asked.

"Yes, this is Miranda Moon."

"Please hold for Timothy Lufti."

"Sure." Miranda wrapped her arms around herself, desperately wishing that she'd remember to bring her coat with her. It was inside the restaurant, hanging on the back of her chair. If Tim took any longer to arrive on his own phone call, she was going to turn into a popsicle.

"Miranda?" Tim asked. "You there?"

"Yeah, Tim. Still here," she said a little testily.

"Sorry about that. My daughter called with a minor emergency and—"

"It's okay. You don't have to explain," she said, softening her tone. He'd already proven to be worth his salt. Earlier in the week she'd finally gotten her payments from her former agent, though Olivia still hadn't called. And at that point, Miranda didn't expect or even want her to. She had her money and a lawyer doing the work she needed him to do. "Do you have any news about the movie?"

"Yes. The script is being overnighted to you. I know you read Silas's version. There have apparently been a few changes since then, though they say nothing major. You have seven days to submit your notes. The producer was quick to inform me that with the contract you signed they aren't obligated to use any of your changes. Their only obligation is to consider them."

"Right," she said, resigned. "We already knew that, though I suppose this means they are driving the point home that they don't care what I think."

"Probably, but this way by giving you a deadline before they start filming, they are making a case that they will consider your notes. It's a smart move for them. They also say that they sent a note to your former agent two months ago letting her know that the script would be made available to you should you still want input. Since Olivia isn't answering our calls, there is no way to know if that's true or not."

"Freakin' Olivia." Miranda wouldn't put it past her. Her agent had been really angry when Miranda decided to independently publish her work. It was the best career move for Miranda, but it meant Olivia ended up without a cut of her normal advance. It had made Miranda sad that she'd just

ESSENCE OF THE WITCH

been seen as a paycheck to her longtime agent, but money did strange things to people.

"There's more," Tim said, sounding hesitant.

"What is it?" Miranda was at full attention now and so focused on the call she didn't even feel the cold anymore.

"We found out who is producing the movie, and it's quite strange considering your contract is with Witching Hour Productions. Do you know who Throm Alexander is?"

Her heart sped up and thudded against her ribcage at the mention of Gideon's father. "Yeah. He owns Ace Media."

"Right," Tim confirmed. "But for some reason, he appears to be the financial backer behind this movie and the sole producer. I'm told he personally hired the screenwriter and director. It seems as if all decisions lead back to him, which, as I'm sure you know, is highly unusual for this type of deal. Witching Hour seems to have handed him the reins while keeping their name on the masthead."

"That's... insane," Miranda finally choked out. "Throm Alexander hates my book. He tried to kill my publishing deal all those years ago. Why would he want to produce the movie?"

But as soon as the words flew out of her mouth, she knew. Throm got word that her movie was being made and somehow weaseled his way into it so that he could change it. But why? To hurt her? Why did he even care? He'd gotten what he wanted all those years ago. Gideon had walked away from her and straight into his dad's office.

While he'd been trying to get her book pulled from production, Throm had promised her he'd back down and leave the book deal alone as long as she severed contact with Gideon.

The notion had been ridiculous. The thought that she'd

cave to Throm Alexander's demands had made her laugh. She'd called him on his crap and challenged him to try. As much as she'd wanted to be published, she hadn't been willing to sacrifice Gideon for her dreams. But it turned out Gideon had left shortly after that anyway.

Her book had been published, and until earlier that month, she hadn't seen Gideon ever again. Was this the reason Gideon had shown up in Keating Hollow? But again, why? She had no idea, and her head was starting to hurt.

"I don't have any answers as to why Throm Alexander has decided to back your movie, but if there is history there and the material is significantly changed, I might be able to use that if you want to pursue legal action."

"You know I used to date his son, don't you?" she asked.

"I also know you've been seeing him now. Shannon mentioned something about it when we spoke. Nothing personal, just a harmless comment that put the pieces together for me."

"It's fine that you know. It's not a secret," Miranda said, her thoughts whirling. "Listen, Tim, thanks for the information. After I get the script, I'll let you know where I stand. And yes, there is history there. If I decide to move forward, I'll tell you all about it then."

"All right. Don't hesitate to call if you need anything," he said.

"Thanks, Tim. I appreciate your help. And the checks Olivia finally sent."

He chuckled softly. "I'm glad at least that part worked out smoothly."

"Me too."

The second Miranda ended the call with Tim, she called Gideon again. No answer.

188

She slumped against the brick wall of Woodlines and pressed a hand to her aching heart. Had Gideon known? Surely, he would've told her if he had, wouldn't he? Considering he was an executive over at Ace media, it stood to reason that he would know. But if so, why had he kept it from her? If Throm Alexander really did just want to invest in her movie, what was there to hide?

The changed script, the voice in her head said.

Confused and almost numb from the cold, Miranda went back into the restaurant, grabbed her coat, apologized to Cameron for bailing early, and went home to wait for Gideon's call.

CHAPTER 24

*G*ideon walked out of Baker's home office, his fist clutching a folder of paperwork and his jaw aching from clenching his teeth. It had taken every last bit of his willpower to refrain from putting his fist through the investigator's wall. But Baker must've been used to delivering bad news, because before Gideon could lose his ever-loving mind, the man had poured him a shot of whiskey and told him to down it. Gideon had done as he was told and then took deep breaths to calm his worst impulses.

Now that he was out of the house, his vision had turned red again. He briefly thought about calling Miranda, but he was far too angry to talk to anyone. Well, anyone who wasn't his father.

It took him less than fifteen minutes to make the twenty-mile drive to Ace Media. As it turned out, his father actually hadn't left town for the holidays. That had been a lie, right along with so many others he'd just learned about.

Baker's research revealed that Throm's fourth wife had

left him five months ago and that he hadn't been anywhere other than his office or his fortress of a home since. Though a certain budding television star had been seen coming and going from his property at all hours of the day and night. The actress was just out of college and working on her first television show that was produced by Ace Media. That on its own would've been enough to enrage Gideon. With all of the sexual harassment cases in the news, something like that was a recipe for disaster. But at the moment it was a minor side issue.

Jerking his BMW to a stop in his marked parking space in the Ace Media garage, Gideon scowled at the sign. This was the life he'd chosen over Miranda all those years ago? One of money and access and power? All of which he'd never really cared about. But he had wanted to make his father proud. Gain his approval. Prove that he was worthy of his remaining parent's love.

All of that was a joke. His father had lied to him for years. Controlled Gideon to uphold his own reputation. Gideon was just done. But not before he handled a few things first.

His heavy footsteps were loud on the glossy tiled floors and echoed off the walls in the deserted hallway. This close to the holiday, most of the staff had taken vacation already. There were still admins manning the desks, but the executives and senior staff were off at warm beaches or ski slopes, taking a much-needed break.

He rounded a corner and swept into his father's office suite.

Kim jerked her head up from her computer and let out a tiny gasp before collecting herself. She cleared her throat. "Gideon, what are you doing here? I thought you were enjoying some well-deserved time off."

"Where is he?" Gideon pointed to the closed office door. "In there?" Before she managed to answer, he strode to it and yanked the door open. Or he tried to. The door was locked and didn't budge. He spun around. "Just tell me the truth. Is he in there or is he at home?"

"I, um, thought he had plans with your stepmother to go to Belize or something this season," she said, pressing her hand to her throat and glancing at her desk.

"It was Costa Rica," he said dryly. Gideon had never seen Kim so flustered. Usually she was calm and all business. She was a kickass assistant who got the work done and knew how to schmooze to get the contacts and meetings her boss needed. But in that instance, she looked like she wanted no part of the conversation. "That's the rumor, but I have it on good authority that Cherise left him five months ago and he's having a fling with Kimmie Newsome, the fresh-out-of-college blonde that just landed a supporting role on our new hit television show. Did he have something to do with the casting?"

She shook her head *no* and pressed a hand to her stomach as her face turned a pale shade of white. Gideon had the distinct impression she was trying not to vomit, but she forced out, "Mr. Alexander doesn't share any details of his personal life. I wouldn't know about any of that."

He refrained from rolling his eyes. He didn't want to torture Kim. He knew she was just doing her best to not lose her job. "Never mind. Why don't you go deliver a message to Lenora for me?"

She glanced at the phone on her desk and back at him.

Gideon shook his head, grabbed a tablet from her desk, and jotted something down for his own assistant. After he folded it, he handed it to Kim and said, "It's personal."

"Right." Relief flooded her expression, and she hurried to the door. But just before she left, she whispered, "Top right drawer. The one with the blue tag." Then she disappeared.

Gideon strode to her desk, retrieved the key to his father's office, and silently thanked Kim for her help. He would've found a way into the office one way or another, but breaking the door down would've taken a lot more effort than just using the key.

A moment later the lock clicked, and without so much as a knock, Gideon stormed in.

His father didn't even look up as he barked, "Kim, I told you I don't want to be disturbed."

"Kim isn't here," Gideon said, his voice laced with unmistakable rage.

"Gideon?" Throm Alexander jerked his head up to stare at his son. "How did you get in here?"

Gideon scoffed. "Not why are you here? Or what's wrong? Just how did you get in here?"

Throm closed the laptop that sat on his desk and rose from his chair. He was dressed impeccably as usual, but his hair was in need of a trim and he looked as if he hadn't shaved in three days. In other words, for the meticulous Throm Alexander, he was downright disheveled. "I'm just surprised. Are you home to spend the holidays with me and your stepmother? Because she's already in Costa Rica. I stayed behind to finish working on a project. I don't know yet if I'll be able to meet up with her—"

"Cut the crap. I know that Cherise left you and that she isn't in Costa Rica. She's in San Diego living with her mother because you cut her off."

Throm's eyes narrowed. "Where did you hear that?"

"Does it matter, *father*?" he asked. "It's the truth isn't it? Just like it's the truth that she left you because you're having an affair with a certain young actress." His father's philandering and cheating was enough to piss him off on any random day, but it wasn't the real reason he was standing in his father's office shaking. He was still working his way up to the big confrontation.

"My personal life is my business. Cherise wanted to wait until after the holiday to say anything, and I support her choice," his father said stiffly.

It didn't escape Gideon's notice that he hadn't defended himself on the affair accusation. He decided to let that one go and said, "Sure. It's what Cherise wanted. Is she the one who wanted you to single-handedly fund Miranda Moon's movie, *Witching for You*?"

Throm's expression turned completely blank, and Gideon knew that was his father's way of icing him out. "Cherise doesn't have anything to do with my business decisions. You know that."

"Right. Despite the fact that she was a successful director for ten years before you two married, her opinion never was welcome. That's some effed-up shit, Dad. Cherise is going to win an Oscar one day, and you won't have any part of it."

Throm sniffed, dismissing Gideon's statement. "What did you come here for, Gideon?"

Gideon tossed the file on his father's desk and jerked his head at it as the pictures and documents slipped out. "Seems you've been keeping some family secrets."

His father's cool façade disappeared as shock made his eyes widen and his mouth open.

It was an expression Gideon was certain he'd never seen

his father wear before. "I guess we finally know why you really divorced my mother and punished her by keeping her tied up in court for years just because she had the audacity to seek affection you were never willing to give."

"Your mother cheated on me," he said defensively.

Gideon didn't dispute that fact, but he'd always been willing to bet his entire fortune on the fact that his father had cheated first. The man hadn't been faithful to any of his other three wives, so why should his mother have been any different? Sadly, he'd never get her side of the story since she'd passed away over a decade ago. "And the end result of that affair was me, right?"

"So, what if you were? From the moment you were born, you were *my* son. Biology doesn't matter," Throm insisted.

"No? If it doesn't matter, why did you go to such great lengths to pay people off to keep their mouths shut? And why did you work so hard to keep Miranda's book from being published? She doesn't know you're not my blood father. I don't understand why that book was such a threat to you."

The information Baker dug up involved records of payoffs and nondisclosure agreements around some mysterious news story. He'd used his contacts in the industry to finally learn that when Miranda's deal was announced, another reporter had gone all-in on learning about the leading man behind the story. When they learned Gideon was the son of a powerful Hollywood producer, they began digging.

And that's when they found out that Throm wasn't Gideon's biological father. That his mother had cheated on Throm with his best friend. Just before the story was to break, Throm paid a bunch of people off and did everything he could to get Miranda's production deal axed.

In the grand scheme of things, an affair and a secret baby in Hollywood was just another day's news. No one would talk about it for long, but Gideon knew Throm's ego was far too fragile. He wouldn't put up with any sort of humiliation. So he'd done what he always did; he manipulated the situation for his own satisfaction. But Gideon still didn't understand why the book was such a big deal.

Throm's entire body tensed as he curled his hands into fists. "That was an embarrassment Ace Media could not afford to weather back then. Your *girlfriend's* book invited questions I didn't want to answer."

Gideon snorted. "The joke's on you. No one came around asking any questions after it hit the bestseller lists."

Throm's eyebrows raised. "You really think that? Do you want to see the checks I wrote to keep reporters quiet? The records are out there Gideon. Why do you think I divorced your mother? I found out when you were in high school after a routine physical. Blood types don't lie. And health professionals, the unethical kind, talk."

"So you've been spending all kinds of money to keep this secret. Why? I don't really get it. Mom is gone. I'm a grown-ass man. I've been working for Ace for fifteen years. What difference does it make? Is your ego that fragile—"

"Don't be so naïve, Gideon," he snapped, his eyes going slightly wild. "Your mother cheated to get back at me for my... ah, indiscretions. A few of them ended in false accusations, one in particular with a moderately powerful politician's daughter. If that came out... Ace would've been ruined. I did what I had to do."

"False accusations? What does that mean?" Gideon felt

sick to his stomach. Was his father trying to tell him he had his own *#metoo* scandal just waiting to break? "What did you do?" he demanded.

"Nothing. I've only ever been in consensual situations. But when you have money and power, sometimes women lie. You know how it is."

"No, I don't know how it is, *Dad*." He wanted to bolt, get as far away from this man as possible. All of the lies and justifications and doubts were too overwhelming. "So this was always about protecting you and your problematic sexual exploits. It has nothing to do with the fact that I'm not biologically your son."

"It's both. Those are scandals we don't need."

"So you've said. Is that why you've changed the script for *Witching for You* so much? So that the story will be more about Cory than me, and there will be less chance of people trying to dig into my family history?"

"Yes. This has always been about protecting what is ours," he said. "If Miranda hadn't written a book about you, none of this would've been necessary."

"You mean if you hadn't harassed a politician's daughter none of this would've been necessary," Gideon countered.

"I didn't harass anyone," Throm shouted. "See? This is exactly why none of those accusations can come out. My own son doesn't even believe me."

Gideon stared at the man he'd wanted to please his entire life and just felt disgusted. It wasn't a huge leap to believe he'd been inappropriate with women. The man was a powerful Hollywood executive. There was a culture of women and money and power. His father had been at the helm of it for years. In fact, he'd heard his share of inappropriate comments from the man over the years and cringed every time. What had happened behind closed doors, Gideon couldn't say, but one thing he did know was that Throm Alexander always expected to get whatever he wanted. "Just tell me one thing."

"What?" Throm asked, sounding tired.

"Why didn't you just buy the film rights to *Witching for You* and then bury it? Why produce it as something it isn't?"

"Believe me, I tried. But Miranda wouldn't let us buy the rights. I bid for them numerous times. And Witching Hour was going to go ahead with or without me, so I put up all the money in order to get control. And Miranda's contract with Witching Hour doesn't allow her any influence about the content or the production."

Gideon shook his head. "You've really made a mess for yourself. What exactly do you think is going to happen if this news breaks?"

Throm sat back in his chair and ran a nervous hand through his salt-and-pepper hair. "You've seen what happens these days with these kinds of accusations. Ace Media will be blackballed."

"You mean *you'll* be blackballed," Gideon said, pressing both hands down on his father's desk. "Listen to me and listen carefully. I'm officially resigning from Ace Media today unless you step down, effective immediately."

"What?" Throm stood so quickly his chair toppled over behind him. "You can't threaten me. Ace Media is *my* company."

"Technically, it's *our* company." Gideon had earned a substantial amount of stock shares on his ten-year anniversary with the company. But he didn't care about that. He cared about the employees and wanted to make sure they didn't lose their jobs when his father was exposed. Because he had no doubt that eventually he would be.

"I'm not resigning," Throm insisted.

"Fine. Then I quit. Good luck." He started to move toward the door but then stopped and turned back to his father. "Withdraw your investment in *Witching for You*, or I'll go to the press myself."

His father's face turned bright red, and Gideon was certain steam would start shooting out of his head at any moment. "You *will not* do that."

"How are you going to stop me this time? Miranda's movie is happening whether either of us want it to or not. And I'm quitting anyway. I just don't see the leverage."

"I'll find a way to smear your girlfriend's name," he threatened.

That rage that Gideon had finally contained came roaring back. "If you even think about doing that, the war is on. I'll call everyone I know in the media and give interviews for the next two years. This will never end, and eventually your accusers will stream out of the woodwork. Stay away from me and Miranda, and we'll stay away from you. That's the deal."

"I'll cut you off," Throm said.

Gideon let out a full-throated laugh. He couldn't care less. "I have my own money. I don't need yours."

"I have ten times your wealth," his father insisted.

Gideon shrugged. That was the truth, but what his father never understood was that Gideon just didn't care. All he'd ever really wanted was Miranda and, as a young man, his father's approval. He'd done what was expected of him back then. Now he was doing what was right. "Keep it. I don't want it."

Without another word, he strode out of his father's office, took a few moments to warn Kim and Lenora that they might want to look for new employment before the shit hit the fan, and then made a few calls to start his transition from Hollywood to Keating Hollow. It was time to go home to Miranda.

CHAPTER 25

*M*iranda paced her small cottage and idly wondered if it was actually possible to wear a path in the floor. Gideon had been gone for three days, and all she'd gotten were a couple of texts letting her know he was wrapping something up and that he'd be back in Keating Hollow as soon as possible.

"What the hell does 'as soon as possible' mean?" she asked no one. "Four days? Two weeks? Six months?" She let out a groan and ran up the stairs to drown out her thoughts under the hot spray of the shower.

When she was dressed, hair done, and makeup applied, she looked at her phone for the thousandth time that day and wanted to throw it across the room when there weren't any new messages. She needed to get out of the cabin. If she were a stronger woman, she'd leave the phone behind so she'd stop staring at it, but there were still some details to be worked out for the Christmas ball, and she didn't want to miss any calls.

Bundled in her wool coat, fur-lined boots, and matching hat and scarf, she made her way outside to her Mercedes. The snow was long gone, but the temperatures had stayed just above freezing, which was somewhat unusual for Keating Hollow in December, or so she'd been told.

On the way to town, she called Cameron. He was staying in Keating Hollow until it was time to start filming his next movie, and the two had become close. Writing and selling a television script together would do that to people.

"What's up?" he said when he answered. "Has your man shown up yet?"

"No," she huffed out. "And I need some muscle. Can you meet me at the Pelshes' winery? I want to get started on the decorations."

He let out a fake huff of annoyance. "This is what it's come to, huh? I'm your backup? What if I strain a muscle? Are you going to massage it for me? Kiss it and make it better?"

"Shut up," she ordered. "If you break yourself, I'll make you an appointment at the spa. Can you meet me or not?"

"Yeah. Sure. But bring me a double latte. I need a pick-me-up," he said.

"I'll do better than that. I'll bring pastries, too."

"Did I ever tell you how much I love you, Miranda Moon?" he teased.

"Yep. Yesterday when I gave you my coffee cake. I like that your needs are pretty simple. Pastries and caffeine. We're a match made in heaven, where we both weigh twice our fighting weight."

He chuckled. "But we'll be burning calories today, so it's fine. Even better than fine. It's almost mandatory."

She rolled her eyes, even though he couldn't see her, and said, "I'm stopping at Incantation Café now. See you in fifteen."

With coffee and treats in hand, Miranda made her way into the event hall at the Pelsh winery. It was a large, open space designed to be used for weddings and other large parties. It conveniently had a kitchen at one end and dressing rooms at the other. The decorations had already been started, and thousands of sparkling stars hung down from the ceiling.

The tree was the big thing she wanted to get done that day. It was also the one thing she hadn't been willing to delegate. She had specific ideas of what she wanted it to look like. Elegance was mandatory, but she also wanted it to feel personalized for the town.

Miranda disappeared into one of the dressing rooms and found the bags she was looking for. The decorations had all been delivered earlier in the week, but she hadn't had the time or the will to do anything about it. Since the ball was just a couple of days away, it was time to stop procrastinating.

When she returned to the ballroom, she spotted Cameron eyeing the progress. Red cloth-covered tables had been set up around the perimeter of the room. The vases for the centerpieces were there, but the Christmas bouquets wouldn't show up until the day of the event. A mural had been painted on one of the walls that depicted the town in all its Christmas glory, and the snowmen were already in place, though they had yet to be spelled to dance on their own. There was no need to expend that much energy when it could be done the night before.

"Hey," she said, nodding to the latte in his hand. "Looks like you found your fuel."

He grinned. "It was like a homing beacon. I swear, I walked in without any conscious thought and went straight for it."

"Right. I'm sure it helped that it was on the table closest to the door," she said, handing him one of the bags. "Come on, muscles. Let's get to work."

After downing his latte and eating two slices of coffee cake, Cameron started to help Miranda put the small, framed-picture ornaments on the tree. Each one was a recent picture of one of the town's businesses all spruced up for the holiday.

"This is a nice touch," Cameron said. "I bet the business owners and residents are going to love this."

"I hope so. I'm pretty much the resident newbie, so I'm kinda flying by the seat of my pants here and trying to decide what might win them over."

"I think as long as you provide booze and Christmas cookies, you likely can't go wrong," he said with a wink.

He was probably right, but Miranda was still nervous about planning the ball without much input. The committee had helped make the big decisions like where to hold the event, but beyond that, they'd left it in her hands. What could she say? She just wanted to make a good impression.

They spent the next few hours decorating the giant tree, and Miranda was just about ready to call it a day when she heard footsteps behind her.

"Hey, you," a familiar male voice said.

Her skin tingled the way it always did when Gideon was near. She spun around, spotted him, and immediately threw her arms around him. "You're back!"

He gathered her up and held her close, almost as if he'd been desperate to get her back into his arms. She loved that he didn't have any reservations, and she pressed her lips to his neck, just happy to have him home.

Home. Had she really just thought that? He'd never said he was moving to Keating Hollow. But damn, she wanted that. She wanted it more than she'd ever wanted anything.

"I have news," she blurted as she pulled back.

"So do I," he said, smiling down at her. "But you go first."

She grinned up at him and then cast a glance over her shoulder. "Cameron got us a deal for our television series. It's supposed to go into production sometime next year. If it gets a good reception, they want a season two."

His face lit up with excitement. "That's wonderful, Mandy. Who ordered the shows?"

"Only the number one streaming service in the country," she said, beaming with pride. "Can you believe it?"

"Yes," he said simply. "You're brilliant."

She shrugged one shoulder, trying to appear humble. "Nothing would've happened without Cameron. He had the connections and the experience with script writing."

"The story and most of the arc were her ideas," Cameron called from his perch on a ladder where he was still hanging gold ornaments on the tree.

"Congratulations," Gideon said, cupping her cheek and bending his head to give her a soft kiss. "You deserve this."

"Thank you." She pressed her palms to his chest and narrowed her eyes slightly as she asked, "And what news do you have? What took so long?"

He cleared his throat and took a step back. "We should talk in private."

All of the happiness that had consumed her at seeing him vanished. "That sounds ominous."

"No, nothing like that. It's about my father." His words were clipped, but she knew his mood had everything to do with whatever was going on with his father and not anything she'd said or done.

"Did you get my message about him financing *Witching for You?*" she asked.

"Yeah, about that. That's why I went back to Los Angeles—"

"Wait," she said, cutting him off and taking a couple of steps backward. "You knew?"

"Yes, but—" he tried again.

"When did you know?" she demanded, her hackles up and dread seeping into her consciousness.

"Um, the day you hired Timothy. I called the office and—"

"You've known for two weeks!" she cried. "And you didn't tell me?" He opened his mouth to say something, but she held her hand up, stopping him. "No. Never mind. I don't want to hear this. You kept this vital information from me. I had to hear about it from my lawyer while you knew all along. That's not how real relationships work, Gideon. Gods! After all these years, I thought maybe you were done being your father's lap dog, but I guess I got that all wrong, didn't I?"

"That's not what happened," Gideon said, his jaw tight with frustration. "I can explain."

She placed her hands on her hips, cocked her head to the side, and said, "Well? I'm waiting."

Gideon blew out a breath and ran an unsteady hand through his dark locks. "I was waiting to tell you until I figured out why he was backing the movie. I didn't want you to stress about him and what he was doing until we had more information."

"So you just cut me out as if I couldn't handle it. Is that right?"

"It's not that I didn't think you could handle it. I just..." He trailed off and shrugged his shoulders as if he didn't know what he was trying to say. "I just wanted answers first."

"So *you* could try to handle it?" she asked, practically spitting the words at him. The amount of rage and frustration consuming her was so overwhelming that she thought her head might actually explode. When he'd left her fifteen years ago, he hadn't been honest with her then either. He'd told Miranda he was letting her go so she could live the life she was meant to live. And he was going to give his life working for the family business, as was always intended. His fantasy of opening a beachside gallery had been nothing but romance. "It's time to grow up, Miranda," he'd said.

"No... well, yes," Gideon admitted. "My father shouldn't be anywhere near this project," he said solemnly. "If there was something I could do to change it, I would. Trust me. I've already made that clear to my father in no uncertain terms. In fact—"

"I've heard enough," Miranda said. "I believe you when you say you'd change this if you could. The problem is that you can't. But the bigger problem is that you don't see me as an equal. You didn't confide in me, just like you didn't confide in me when you decided to go work for your father all those years ago."

Gideon's brow furrowed as he stared at her. "What do you mean?"

She rolled her eyes. "Did you really think I didn't know

about the deal you two made? You'd work for him if he left my book deal alone."

"How did you know that?"

"He told me, Gideon. When he threatened me. He told me never to mention you or talk about you to the press. Otherwise, he'd sue me into oblivion just because he could. Money buys you lawyers even when the case is groundless."

"He threatened you?" Gideon asked, but then his features hardened almost immediately. "Of course he did. That bastard."

"The point is, Gideon, you didn't talk to me then and you didn't talk to me this time. We have a connection, but I've never wanted a savior. I can't be a part of something where I'm not a true partner. You should've discussed things with me. Both times. I deserve that much respect."

"You're right. You did and you do," he said, shoving his hands into his pockets. "Can we start over?"

"No. I think it's better if we let this go. Your life is in LA anyway. Let's not make this harder than it has to be," she said, praying that her heart wouldn't break in two. As angry as she was about the situation, she did love him. She could forgive him keeping stuff from her because he thought he was protecting her, but she needed to just end this. She'd been living in a fantasy. It was time to wake up and move on.

"What if my life wasn't in LA anymore?" he asked, studying her. "What if I moved here?"

She let out a bark of hysterical laughter. "You're not moving here. What would you do? Host indie movie showings at Yvette's bookstore?"

"I have a few ideas," he said, moving closer.

She let him, and when he was just inches away, she pressed her hand to his cheek and said, "I'm sorry, Gideon. I just can't do this again. It was hard the first time. This time might break me."

His eyes bored into hers, and she could tell he was going to continue to try to talk her out of her decisions, but the tears were building behind her eyes and she had to get out of there. Turning on her heel, she spun and strode out of the building without looking back.

CHAPTER 26

*G*ideon hadn't spoken to Miranda in a couple of days. He'd called and apologized to her voicemail and asked her to call him when she was ready. Then he'd ordered himself to give her space. He understood that she'd pulled away because she didn't trust that he was ready to leave Los Angeles or defy his father enough to actually walk away. She'd learn soon enough though, because he was in Keating Hollow for good.

His house down south was already on the market, and his assistant Lenora was working on getting his personal things boxed and in storage until he could find a place to live. She'd taken his advice and gave notice just after Gideon left, but because Throm was an ass of epic proportions, he'd let her go on the spot. When Lenora called for a reference, he'd asked her to work for him in the interim until she found something permanent.

"Gideon!" a vivacious redhead called as she strode across Incantation Café, exuding confidence. "There you are. For some reason I thought we were meeting outside. Sorry I'm late. I got caught up chatting with Abby Townsend."

He stood and held out his hand to Wanda Danvers, the town's only real estate agent. "It's all right. I'm not in a hurry."

"Thanks, but I do at least try to be professional when I'm working." She grinned and took a seat across from him, already pulling a folder out of her messenger bag. "Unfortunately, we don't have a lot on the market right now. Just a couple of rentals and two homes for sale. None of them meet your specifications, but I figured I'd show them to you just in case you're interested in something temporary until something comes on the market or you decide to build."

"Build?" he said stupidly. He hadn't said anything about being interested in a custom home.

"You don't want to build?" she asked curiously. "There are lots up in the hills that feature incredible views of the valley. Both Brian and Jacob built up there recently. It's pretty incredible. But if dealing with contractors isn't your thing, we'll find you something… eventually."

Gideon wasn't exactly a stranger to construction. His house down south had been a custom build. And under other circumstances, he'd have been fine with considering that approach in a town that was growing and so limited on housing. The problem was that he wanted to live with Miranda in her perfect cottage on the edge of the trees. If she wanted to build something larger for the two of them, he'd be on board, but her place was so perfect for her that he couldn't imagine her living anywhere else.

Not that she seemed interested in sharing her space with him. She wasn't even talking to him at the moment.

He sucked in a breath and blew it out just to clear his

head. "I'm not necessarily opposed to building, but I think I want to live here for a bit before I make any long-term decisions."

"A rental then," she said decisively. "I've got two, but curb your expectations. Neither are anything close to updated."

Gideon shrugged. "I appreciate your candor, but how bad could they be?"

She snorted as she led him outside and to her sparkly purple golf cart. "Don't say I didn't warn you."

"We're taking this?" he asked as he climbed in beside her. "Isn't it a little cold out here for that?"

She just grinned and flipped a switch. Immediately the seats started to warm.

"I see. That's a great feature."

ASKING how bad the rentals could be had been a mistake. Because bad was an understatement. The first two-bedroom Wanda showed him was drafty, had shoddy electrical, and the kitchen sink leaked. If that wasn't enough, the place smelled like moldy cheese.

"I think we can safely say this one's a no," he told Wanda.

"I don't blame you." She guided him back to her golf cart, blasted the seat warmers and the music, and zipped down the street to the next showing.

The second one had holes in the linoleum, squirrels living in the roof, and smelled like cat urine. "I find it hard to believe that these places even pass regulations," Gideon said.

"Me too, honestly. But it's probably been a while since an inspector has been out. I'm sorry. I did try to warn you."

He couldn't argue with that. "All right. Show me the ones for sale."

"You got it." They motored into another, nicer neighborhood, and Gideon started to feel encouraged. The first one was a two bedroom-one bath old-style Victorian. It hadn't been updated since the seventies but appeared to be in somewhat-decent shape structurally. The second one was a two bedroom-two bath that had a different paint color in each room and olive-green appliances as well as bathroom fixtures. But it had great built-ins and a lovely view from the back porch that overlooked the river.

"This one," he said. "Do you know of a decent contractor for remodeling?"

"Sure. Hunter McCormick, Faith Townsend's husband. He comes highly recommended. Great work and reasonable prices."

"Sounds perfect." He glanced around at the layout of the house and decided that, no matter what happened, it would be a good investment. "Let's get the paperwork started."

"That was a fast decision," Wanda said, eyeing him. "I don't want to shoot myself in the foot or anything, but are you sure you don't want to sleep on it?"

"I'm sure," he said decisively. "Even if I decide I don't want to live in *this* house, it looks like a solid investment."

"You're not wrong about that," she said, beaming. "Back to the coffee shop? I can get the offer done on my computer while we warm up with some Irish coffees."

"Hanna sells alcohol there?" he asked, sure he hadn't seen that on the menu.

"Nope. But there's a bottle of Irish cream stashed in the back." She winked at him, and together they hopped back into the party cart. Wanda blasted Prince through the built-in speakers and danced in her seat the entire way back to Main Street.

Wanda hadn't been kidding about the Irish cream. Once they had their coffees in hand, she grabbed both cups and disappeared into the back. When she reappeared, she was grinning and clearly pleased with herself. "Just don't spread that little bit of info around. We don't want to get Hanna into any trouble."

"I'm a vault," he said and sat back in his chair while Wanda worked her magic.

"Gideon," Cameron Copeland said, striding up to the table.

Gideon glanced up at the man who towered over their table. "Hey, Cameron. What can I do for you?"

"Can we talk for a moment?" Cameron glanced at Wanda, who was eyeing him with interest.

"Well, hello there," Wanda said and held out her hand. "I hear you're pretty good with your pen."

"That's what I'm told," he said, his eyes glinting with amusement. "And what are you good at?"

She grinned. "That's kind of a personal question, don't you think?"

Cameron laughed. "I suppose so. Are you going to answer it?"

Shrugging, she said, "I'm a great real estate agent, a top-shelf golf cart racer, and if I like you, I'm the best date in town."

"I just bet you are," Cameron said, scanning his gaze over her body. "It's short notice, but do you have a date to the ball tonight?"

"I was going to go solo. Keep my options open. But if you're offering to get me a corsage and take me to dinner first, I'm not going to say no."

"Yes to dinner, but I don't know about the corsage. Is that

a deal-breaker?" he asked.

Wanda laughed. "No. But you would be crushing my high school-prom fantasy. I never got to go because I was sick."

"Corsage it is." They exchanged numbers and set a time all while Gideon watched in awe at their blatant flirting and easy banter. Had he and Miranda been like that when they'd first met? No. Definitely not. They'd met in a coffee shop much like the Incantation Café. Miranda had worked there, and while she'd flirted with him, it had taken him a while to loosen up and go with it. He admired the way Wanda and Cameron were so at ease with each other even though they hadn't met before.

"Gideon?" Cameron said again. "Ready?"

Gideon stood and followed the man to another table, and they sat across from each other. Gideon clasped his hands together and waited to find out what the man had to say.

"Did you have anything to do with the offer that came through for me this morning?" Cameron asked.

"What offer?" he asked, genuinely out of the loop.

"It's for the *Witching for You* script. The previous screenwriter was let go, and now they want me to fix it."

Gideon beamed. He had no idea what had gone down since he'd stormed out of his father's office, but if Cameron was taking over the script, everything with the movie was going to turn out just fine. He might be a tiny bit jealous that Miranda spent so much time with him now that they were working together, but he knew Cameron was a brilliant screenwriter. Whatever he did with it, the movie was sure to be Oscar material. "No, I didn't have anything to do with it, but I'm glad they hired you. It's what the movie deserves."

"Thanks, man," Cameron said.

Gideon expected him to move on once he had the answer

to his question, but instead, he eyed Gideon with curiosity. "What?" Gideon asked.

"When are you going to tell her you're staying here?"

Gideon knew he was talking about Miranda. There was no reason to clarify. "Just as soon as she's ready to talk. I left her a message. Now I'm giving her space."

Cameron leaned forward on his elbows. "Listen, between you and me, she's had quite enough space. She misses you."

Sighing, Gideon leaned back. "I don't want to push her. She'll figure out soon enough that I'm here to stay. I'm buying a house near the river. That should convince her."

"Interesting." He stood and peered down at Gideon. "Well, our girl doesn't have a date for the ball, and it would be a damned shame if no one spun her around the dance floor after all that work she's done." He gave Gideon a cocky smile and added, "See you later, man."

As soon as Cameron disappeared out into the cold, Gideon pulled out his phone and made a call. "Baker? What's the word on my father? Did he pull out of the *Witching for You* production?"

"You don't know?" Baker asked.

"I only know they hired Cameron Copeland to fix the script. My father and I aren't exactly on speaking terms."

Baker chuckled. "Damn, man. You really are out of the loop. A story broke two days ago. Your old man was caught with his pants down with that young new star. She's claiming abuse of power. Witching Hour shoved him out and they're looking for new investors. But since your girl signed a deal with Cameron Copeland last week, it hasn't been an issue. Everyone in the industry is vying for a piece of it."

Gideon felt both intense relief for Miranda but also trepidation about his father. He wondered who leaked the story. Probably one of the admins. Or the actress herself. It was sort of ironic that his dad had spent so much time trying to bury the past when it was his current actions that were threatening to take him down.

"There's talk of him stepping down and you taking over the company," Baker added.

Gideon scoffed. "That's wishful thinking. I'm done in Hollywood. But there's someone I know over at Ace that would do an excellent job. I'll put in a word for him with the board."

"Name?" Baker demanded.

"Penn Lister. Why?"

"I'll run a background scan on him. If he doesn't have too many skeletons in the closet, then you can recommend him."

Gideon chuckled. "You're good to have around, you know that?"

"Yep. But you probably won't be singing my praises when you get the bill."

"Probably not," Gideon agreed.

"I'll be in touch," Baker said.

Once the call ended, Gideon rejoined Wanda and said, "Let's get me a house."

CHAPTER 27

*M*iranda listened to Gideon's message for what seemed like the hundredth time. He was so sweet, apologetic, and self-aware enough to realize she needed space to sort out how she was feeling. And for two days, he'd done just that. Two days of silence.

Frankly, it just pissed her off.

She actually wanted him to fight for her. Groaning, she put her phone down on the table and reached for another Christmas cookie.

"You're gonna have to ask catering to make more of those if you keep that up," Cameron said, walking into the room with all the enchanted presents at the Pelshes' winery. The last thing to do before the party was to put the presents beneath the chairs at the dinner tables. The place resembled an elegant magazine spread. The snowmen had been spelled and were already twirling around the dance floor, the animated fairies were sprinkling their fairy dust from the beams on the open-air ceiling, and the snow was coming down in soft flakes that vanished the moment they landed on something.

It was, quite simply, a magical wonderland.

"Make more of what?" Miranda mumbled as she chewed around the cookie.

Cameron laughed and sat down next to her at the worktable. "Those cookies you don't even realize you're eating."

She glanced at the headless reindeer and groaned. "Dammit. How am I going to fit into my dress after binging these things? I swear the devil made me do it."

"You just keep telling yourself that." He winked and pulled up a chair. "I have news."

"About?" she asked, pleased to have someone to talk to who might take her mind off Gideon.

"I've been contracted to rewrite the screenplay for *Witching for You*," he said.

Miranda blinked at him. "What?"

His lips twitched into a small smile.

"If you're messing with me, I'm going to punch you in the face." Miranda jumped out of her chair and started pacing due to her pent-up energy.

"That's kind of violent, Miranda. You sure that's what you want to lead with considering I'll be writing your story?"

"You... you tell me right now. Is this a joke?" she demanded.

He pulled his phone out of his pocket and opened the email from his agent with the attached contract. "Read it for yourself."

She grabbed his phone. Sure enough, he had been asked to rewrite the screenplay. The previous writer had been let go. "I don't understand. I thought Throm Alexander had control. He'd never give you this after he learned we were working together."

"Throm's dropped out. Witching Hour wasn't pleased with his *values*. I'm sure you saw the story."

Miranda just nodded. She'd been trying not to think of Gideon's dad. It just wasn't good for her mental state. "Seriously? He's out, and you're going to write the screenplay?" Tears filled her eyes and she didn't bother to try to hold them back. "I can't believe this. It's a dream come true." She threw her arms around him and hugged him tightly. "Do right by us, Cam."

He chuckled into her ear. "There's more, gorgeous."

She pulled back and narrowed her eyes at him. "Are you flirting with me? I already told you I can't be your proper date tonight. I'm too busy."

Cameron threw his head back and laughed. "Don't flatter yourself. I have a date."

"With who?"

"That sassy redhead, Wanda. I asked her today, because I'm classy like that." He smirked.

She chuckled. "I bet Wanda was all over that."

He glanced down at himself. "I sure hope so."

"Stop!" She smacked his arm but then laughed with him. "Good. I'm glad you have a date. And Wanda is a ton of fun. I hope you two hit it off."

"I'm sure we'll have a good time." He sat back in his chair and crossed his arms over his chest. "I have something to ask you."

"If the question is 'where do babies come from,' I'm going to have to insist that you stay celibate until you get a sex-ed class," she teased.

"Funny," he said dryly. "I think you'll want to hear this question."

"Just as long as it's not about Gideon," she said before she could swallow the words.

"It's not, but let's put a pin in that for a moment so I can get this out."

Miranda gazed at him. "Okay, Cam. Shoot."

"Will you co-write the *Witching for You* script with me?"

She froze, unable to process what he'd said. "Say that again."

He gave her a twisted half-smile. "Be my partner while I'm working on *Witching for You*. I want your input when I have to make changes."

"Yes!" she cried and flung herself around him. "Yes! Yes! Yes!" Happy tears spilled down her cheeks, and she felt herself start to tremble. With her face buried in his neck, she asked, "Why are you so good to me?"

He squeezed her tighter. "I'm just a sucker for the really good writers. I know I have a reputation for not playing nice with others, but it's because I'm a perfectionist. You, my dear, have a gift that I'm envious of. It's easy to work with someone you admire."

"Oh my goddess," she sobbed. "You're too much." Pulling back, she dabbed at her eyes. "I'm going to be a hot mess tonight if you keep me blubbering."

He nodded. "That was my plan all along. Hot Mess Miranda. It has a certain ring to it, don't you think?"

"Shut it," she ordered and then twirled around. "This is the best day."

"I think there's room for improvement," he said as he winked and walked out of the room.

Miranda didn't know what to make of that statement, but she decided to ignore it. There was too much work to do.

~

FOUR HOURS LATER, Miranda learned what Cameron meant about her day getting better. She was standing near the silent auction table, answering questions about the process, when she spotted him.

Gideon Alexander. The tall man, looking devastatingly handsome in his black-tie suit, had just entered the venue and was headed straight for her.

Miranda smoothed her white corset dress with the sassy red ribbons and prayed she wouldn't act the fool and just throw herself at him. It was a tough call. She had missed him more in the last few days than she had the entire fifteen years they'd been apart the first time. She now knew that their love had never faded, and telling herself they were too young, they weren't compatible, he wasn't made for the lifestyle she wanted... all of that was just garbage.

He was her person and she knew it.

"You look gorgeous, Miranda," Gideon said the moment he reached her side. He placed a box on the table and then turned to stare down at her.

Nervous, she pressed her hands to her waist and said, "That's good, because I didn't squeeze myself into this thing just to be average." She was teasing as she said it, but the way he raked his gaze over her, it was obvious he more than approved. "If you keep looking at me like that, I think the nearest object might just combust."

His gaze darted back to hers and he grinned. "I wouldn't mind a few fireworks to be honest."

"Oh, hell," she breathed. "Let's start over." She pasted a smile on her face and moved in for a quick hug.

Only the hug was far from quick. The moment their arms wrapped around each other, they all but melted into the other one. Damn, he felt good pressed up against her.

"I missed you, Mandy," he whispered as he ghosted tiny kisses over her neck.

"I missed you, too," she admitted.

They were both silent as they clung to each other, until Gideon finally said, "I quit my job."

Miranda pulled back and stared up at him. "You what?"

"I quit. I actually quit the day I came back here, but I didn't get a chance to tell you. My house is already on the market, too. I'm here for good."

Miranda's head spun. She was giddy with happiness while being completely overwhelmed. "Is that why your father backed out of *Witching for You?*"

Gideon shook his head. "I wish I could say I had something to do with that, but it really was Witching Hour who forced him out. His, ah, *image*, doesn't fit their brand."

"I heard about that," she said, squeezing his arm. "Are you okay?"

"I'm perfectly fine, actually. That's his life, not mine. Whatever he did, I hope he pays the price and not that actress. I know how Throm is. It isn't difficult to believe her story." Gideon shrugged as his eyes focused on one of the dancing snowmen that twirled by. Chuckling, he nodded to it. "Those are different."

"They're fantastic. Huge hit. Now back to your dad. What did he do when you quit?"

"Nothing. Nothing much, anyway." Gideon let out a humorless laugh. "He tried to intimidate me, threaten me, cut me off, but all of his threats were meaningless. I don't want the job, his money, or the status. I just wanted to be back here with you."

She sucked in a surprised breath. "He cut you off?"

"I have no idea. It doesn't matter. I have my own money." He tugged her into the middle of the dance floor and wrapped his arms around her waist.

She smiled to herself when she saw Silas and Levi dancing cheek to cheek. They really were an adorable couple, and she was glad to see them looking so happy. Whatever issues they'd been having appeared to have worked out.

"Miranda, listen," Gideon said. "I'm here for good. I even made an offer on a house today."

"You did what?" She stopped swaying to the music and stared at him wide-eyed. "Where?"

"Third Street. It's a fixer-upper, but with some work, I think it will be a cute little place and a decent investment. It overlooks the river."

"I can't believe you're buying a house." But what she really meant to say was that she couldn't believe he was buying a house without her input. If he was going to be in Keating Hollow, there was no doubt in her mind that they'd end up living together. "That's big."

Guh. Her voice sounded full of disappointment even to her own ears.

"Is there a problem with me living here in Keating Hollow?" he asked so softly she barely heard him.

Miranda shook her head. "No. Of course not."

"Then what is it?"

She stared up at the magically falling snow and forced herself to say, "If you really were coming back here for good,

I wanted you to live with me."

"Done," he said simply.

Again, she was speechless. "What do you mean, done?" she finally asked with a laugh.

"I mean done. If you want me to move in with you, I'm there. We can finally get that ending you wrote for us in *Witching for You*."

Miranda's face flushed, but she was also full of pure happiness. Instead of staying true to their story in the book, she'd written the ending she'd wanted, not the one she'd gotten. "How do you feel about a maltipoo?"

"We'll start looking for a puppy to adopt tomorrow," he said, smiling down at her, his eyes full of love.

"You're making my dreams come true, Gideon. But what about that house you're buying? Can you still get out of it if you move in with me?"

"Probably," he said thoughtfully. "But I really do think it's a good investment. I'll move in with you, take some time to fix it up, and then probably rent it out. Or sell it if the price is right. How does that sound to you?"

"It sounds perfect." She buried her head into his chest and held on for all she was worth as they swayed to the ridiculous song, "Grandma Got Run Over by a Reindeer."

When it ended, the clinking of a glass sounded as Abby Townsend stepped up to the mic on the makeshift stage. She was wearing a green velvet dress, had her blond hair piled up in an elegant twist, and was positively radiant. Her husband Clay Garrison was standing just off to the side, beaming at her with stars in his eyes. Miranda sighed. She sure hoped that Gideon gazed at her in adoration the same way Clay gazed at Abby.

"Good evening, everyone. I hope you're all having a grand time!"

A cheer rose up from the crowd.

"That's fantastic. Can we get a round of appreciation for our event chairperson, Miranda Moon?"

This time the cheers were almost deafening, and Miranda could hardly keep from wincing at the noise level. But she felt proud. Her hard work had paid off, and the guests were not only impressed by the event, they were having a fantastic time.

"Excellent. Excellent," Abby called into the microphone. "I agree with you. Miranda did an amazing job."

Abby went on to recognize a number of other people while calling out the winners of the silent auctions, and then she said, "We have one more item to auction tonight, but it's going to be a live auction. How do you feel about that?"

The crowd did not disappoint. They went wild, more than ready to get their bids on.

"Excellent. Let's get our Vanna to bring it out." She waved to Clay, who was nearby with what looked to be a painting in his hands. "We have a special treat for you tonight, folks. It's an original painting by our own Gideon Alexander."

"You've been painting?" Miranda asked him.

He nodded. "Quite a bit, actually."

Miranda turned back to study the painting and let out a gasp as she covered her mouth in surprise. It was a smaller-sized painting, but the detail was exquisite. And she'd know, because it was her portrait, tears rolling down her cheeks, looking completely devastated. It was Miranda at her most vulnerable. And it was stunning. The emotion that he'd captured was so completely beyond words that she couldn't even speak. She just held on to Gideon's hand as the bidding rose higher and higher and higher, until finally, Cameron won the auction by bidding an almost obscene amount of money.

"Well! That went okay, don't you think?" Abby asked the crowd with a chuckle. "I know a lot of you wanted that piece, but you'll have a second chance to own some of Gideon's work. It's being shown at the Enchanted K Gallery on Main Street through the new year. Happy shopping!"

She started to move off the stage but then doubled back, giggling to herself. "Oops. Forgot the biggest news of all." She held her hand out to her husband Clay, who joined her on the stage. Clay raised a champagne glass and gestured for everyone else to follow. Abby held up a glass of ice water. "It appears that Clay finally managed to knock me up. Cheers!"

Miranda let out a gasp at Abby's flippant way of sharing their news. Then she laughed. Gods, she loved Keating Hollow. There was never a dull moment.

She slipped her hand into Gideon's and said, "Your work is at the gallery, huh?"

"Yep. Since yesterday," he confirmed.

"I'll have to check it out. I mean, I can't be living with an artist and not know his work, can I?"

"You know my work," he said dismissively. "Besides, if I move in with—"

"*When* you move in with me. *When*, Gideon."

"Right. When I move in with you, I'm going to need a studio space, so you'll be around to check out my goods anytime you want."

Miranda couldn't help but stare down at the front of his trousers. "You promise?"

He grinned. "It's damned near a requirement at this

point." He glanced around. "How much longer do we need to stay here?"

"We don't. The food has been served, the auctions are completed, and there's a clean-up crew standing by. We can leave any time."

Gideon grabbed her hand and started to lead her toward the exit.

"Eager much?" she teased when they made it outside, bundled in their coats.

"It's been way too long, Miranda. Take me home. Please."

She smiled, pressed her lips to his, and whispered, "Always."

CHAPTER 28

*I*t had been three weeks and five days since Wanda had last been in Cameron Copeland's arms. Ever since that night at the Christmas ball, she hadn't been able to get the man off her mind. They'd had an evening for the record books.

The night had started off light and easy as they bantered back and forth, just enjoying getting to know each other. And then things had turned heated on the dance floor. Who would've guessed that the studious screenwriter would've been such a great dancer?

But he was, and after three songs, she was ready to throw herself at him. She'd refrained, of course. Wanda needed her men to work a little harder than that. So she'd waited him out until he'd growled in her ear and begged to take her back to the Keating Hollow Inn.

The night had been a blur of passion after that, which continued through the holidays and right up until he'd had to take off to go be on-set for the filming of *Witching for You.* Now he was coming back for three days of meetings with

Miranda to go over the rest of the scenes that needed to be filmed.

Eager to see the one man who'd managed to light her up inside in the past ten years, she'd begged Noel to give her a key to Cameron's room so that she could be there to surprise him when he arrived that night.

She bustled around the room, chilling the champagne, turning down the bed, and then slipping into something he wouldn't have too much trouble slipping her out of. Then she waited. And waited. And waited some more. Flights into Eureka were often unpredictable, so she busied herself reading the travel magazine on the nightstand and was quite engrossed in an article about Alaska when she heard the door handle jiggle.

Yes, finally, she said to herself as she ditched the magazine. Positioning herself in a suggestive way that she hoped would drive Cameron insane, she lifted one arm over her head and bit down on her bottom lip.

There were voices in the hall, and Wanda just assumed that it was the bellman Cameron was talking to. But then the door flew open, and two people walked in.

Wanda froze. A man and a woman had just barged in on her in a see-through nightie that covered nothing. *Oh hell*, she thought to herself. But then her eyes locked on an older version of Cameron, and her flight instinct kicked in. She hopped off the bed, trying to pull the impossibly short nightie down as if it would do anything to cover her scantily clad lady bits while she tried to escape, and promptly tripped over the woman's suitcase.

Wanda went down in a heap and let out an *oomph*.

"Mom, Dad, are you two okay?" Cameron called as he

walked into the room. He quickly took stock of the room and then stared at her. "Wanda? What's going on?"

Wanda's brain finally kicked in, and she reached back for the blanket at the end of the bed and wrapped it around herself. "I, um, was trying to surprise you."

He looked between Wanda and the other two people in the room. Then he started to laugh.

"I don't think your friend is amused, dear," the woman said to him.

Cameron wiped tears from his eyes and nodded. "She's not now, but she will be." He smiled at Wanda and then said, "Mom, Dad, meet Wanda. My... friend."

Friend? Friend! Wanda wanted to shout the word at the top of her lungs. Would someone who was just a friend sneak into someone else's hotel room and offer themselves up like Thanksgiving dessert? No. She didn't think so. She and Cameron were not *just friends*.

She'd show him friends.

With her head held high, she grabbed her clothes, retreated to the bathroom, and less than two minutes later, returned fully clothed. "My apologies," she said to Cameron's mother. "I had no idea you were coming with him."

His mother's eyes flashed with amusement just the way that Cameron's often did. "Don't worry, dear. I've done the same thing for his father more times than I can count."

Oh, no. That was just TMI. Wanda cleared her throat. "That's great, Mrs. Copeland. Keeps the passion alive, I suppose."

Why in the hell was Wanda encouraging this conversation? Before Mom could say anything further, Wanda apologized one more time and excused herself from the most awkward situation of her adult life.

"Wanda, wait!" Cameron called as he caught up to her in the hallway. "I'm sorry for laughing."

She shrugged, pretending it didn't matter. "Sorry about that. I had no idea."

"I didn't either to be honest. They decided last minute they wanted to see Keating Hollow."

Wanda nodded. "Sure. I can see that. You have been spending a lot of time here."

He chuckled. "Are you kidding? They don't care about that. They just wanted to see the town that inspired the television series Miranda and I sold."

"Right. Okay. I better go. You have your hands full." She turned to leave but was pulled back into Cameron's arms.

"I'd rather have my hands full of you," he said nuzzling her neck.

"I'm sure that's true," she said, "but I'd better just be on my way. I wouldn't want anyone to get the idea that we're anything more than *friends*."

"Oh, dammit," he muttered, running his hand through his hair.

"Goodnight, Cameron," she said softly and then left the inn with Cameron staring after her.

236

DEANNA'S BOOK LIST

Witches of Keating Hollow:
Soul of the Witch
Heart of the Witch
Spirit of the Witch
Dreams of the Witch
Courage of the Witch
Love of the Witch
Power of the Witch
Essence of the Witch
Muse of the Witch

Witches of Christmas Grove:
A Witch For Mr. Holiday
A Witch For Mr. Christmas

Jade Calhoun Novels:
Haunted on Bourbon Street
Witches of Bourbon Street
Demons of Bourbon Street

Angels of Bourbon Street
Shadows of Bourbon Street
Incubus of Bourbon Street
Bewitched on Bourbon Street
Hexed on Bourbon Street
Dragons of Bourbon Street

Pyper Rayne Novels:
Spirits, Stilettos, and a Silver Bustier
Spirits, Rock Stars, and a Midnight Chocolate Bar
Spirits, Beignets, and a Bayou Biker Gang
Spirits, Diamonds, and a Drive-thru Daiquiri Stand
Spirits, Spells, and Wedding Bells

Ida May Chronicles:
Witched To Death
Witch, Please
Stop Your Witchin'

Crescent City Fae Novels:
Influential Magic
Irresistible Magic
Intoxicating Magic

Last Witch Standing:
Bewitched by Moonlight
Soulless at Sunset
Bloodlust By Midnight
Bitten At Daybreak

Witch Island Brides:
The Wolf's New Year Bride

The Vampire's Last Dance
The Warlock's Enchanted Kiss
The Shifter's First Bite

Destiny Novels:
Defining Destiny
Accepting Fate

Wolves of the Rising Sun:
Jace
Aiden
Luc
Craved
Silas
Darien
Wren

Black Bear Outlaws:
Cyrus
Chase
Cole

Bayou Springs Alien Mail Order Brides:
Zeke
Gunn
Echo

ABOUT THE AUTHOR

New York Times and USA Today bestselling author, Deanna Chase, is a native Californian, transplanted to the slower paced lifestyle of southeastern Louisiana. When she isn't writing, she is often goofing off with her husband in New Orleans or playing with her two shih tzu dogs. For more information and updates on newest releases visit her website at deannachase.com.

Made in the USA
Las Vegas, NV
19 March 2022